CHARLIE'S ANGELS:

A Polyamorous Affair

PENNY BLACWRITE

For Shyann ...
The first girl I ever loved.

PENNY BLACWRITE'S CATALOG

NOTE TO READER

Polygamy and polyamory are two different forms of relationships. Polygamy means that one person, usually a man is married to multiple people. Polygamy is a marital structure that is legal in many Muslim countries where it is common for a man to take more than one wife. In some African countries, even women take more than one husband, but in America, polygamy has been outlawed with the Morrill Anti- Bigamy Law of 1862. Due to ignorance, many people conflate polygamy with polyamory, where polyamory is simply the act of having intimate relationships with more than one person at the same time, which doesn't mean all three parties have to be involved together. Polygamy started in African villages as a form of protection for widows and was rooted in communalism and kingdom building. This ideology has been adopted to polyamory "throuples" and usually used as a ploy for men to coax women into participating in threesomes and sister wife "situation ships" that aren't governed by the law in America.

Let me make this clear. I do not condone poly relationships that are not rooted in kingdom building. I do not condone this new-age form of polyamory that is solely rooted in sexual pleasure and greed, so while this book is full of erotica, it's really rooted in progressive love and radical acceptance. This book is dedicated to Kenya and Carl Stevens who are also Howard University alumni like me. I was introduced to Kenya and Carl via their Butterfly Facebook Group back in 2012 where I learned all about their open marriage and the idea behind their movement, the Progressive Love Academy.

This couple has been featured on Dr. Phil and all across the internet because of their unique open marriage. Carl Stevens allowed his wife to have a boyfriend for years and now all three of them cohabitate together. They taught me about the equality and openness that exists in progressive love, and I wanted to showcase what true polygamy looks like through the lens of radical acceptance and progressive love. I hope you read with an open mind and enjoy it.

PLAYLIST

"He Had It Coming"- Cell Block Tango (Chicago)

"Roleplay"- Trey Songz

"Girl"- Destiny's Child

"Cater to You"- Destiny's Child

 "Bossy"- Kelis ft. Too Short

"Slut Me Out (Remix)"- NLE Choppa ft. Sexy Red

"Needed Me"- Rihanna

"I Just Want It to Be Over"- Keyshia Cole

"Material Girl"- Madonna

"Caught Out There"- Kelis

"Angel in Disguise"- Brandy

 "Runaway Love"- Ludacris ft. Mary J. Blige

"So Beautiful"- Musiq Soulchild

"Lovers & Friends"- Lil Jon ft. Usher & Ludacris

"Moist" Janet Jackson

"Speechless"- Beyonce

"W.A.P."- Cardi B ft. Megan Thee Stallion

"Big Ole Freak"- Megan Thee Stallion

"Just a Friend"- Mario

"Love of My Life"- Erykah Badu ft. Common

"Best Thing I Never Had"- Beyonce

"Baby Mama"- Fantasia

1
MASCULINITY
CHARLESTINA "CHARLIE" THOMPSON

IT WAS ANOTHER LONG, AND TIRESOME DAY WHERE THE balls of my feet were swollen, and the bits of my ankles were tender from a busy shift at work. Despite the fact that my body gave out, my anger was at its pinnacle as soon as I stepped inside my apartment to find none other than Rodney. His face was drenched with defeat, painting a pitiful picture that I was tired of seeing. I used to feel sorry for him, but now he simply repulsed me.

Stepping over trash as I made my way into the living room, loud and obnoxious sounds blared from the TV. *All I wanted was some peace and quiet. Was that too much to ask?*

As I gazed around the dimly lit and equally dreary apartment, a feeling of heaviness invaded my body. *I used to love this place.* I used to love coming home to Rodney. In the beginning when I didn't mind sharing my spacious Lower East Side apartment with him, life was sweet, and light-hearted and jovial vibes awaited me behind the front door every day. We loved each-other genuinely, instead of simply tolerating one another. I miss the days when we got along, when he gave a damn, and when he'd gladly go above and beyond to please me. Nowadays it seemed like anything was too much for me to ask of him. Irritated, I roared as soon as we met each other's countenance.

"Rodney, why do I continuously have to nag you about cleaning up behind yourself, cutting the lights off so our electric bill that I pay isn't skyrocket high, or stressing you about grooming yourself? You're a grown-ass man!" I barked as I rubbed my hands down my face, completely frustrated. I was tired of repeating myself over and over like a damn record player. "I only have one child and he's twenty-one years old, in college, and self-sufficient. I don't have to argue with Jaden about basic shit nearly as much as I have to with you!" It seemed like I constantly had to teach this thirty-seven-year-old good-for-nothing ass nigga how to be a man. I was drained.

Rodney sat lackadaisically across the couch with dark espresso-hued skin and brushed out waves that used to spin when I first met him. Five foot ten inches tall, he was much more attractive when we first met three years prior. But sadly, had since then let himself go, all across the board. First off, he was losing his hair and even had to go as far as getting one of those man weave applications. It looked good for the first two weeks but shortly after it would start lifting like a bad wig. Secondly, he was growing a beer belly from all the fucking yeast he packed on from drinking eight Angry Orchards every day after work. And lastly, his athlete's foot was stinking up my fucking house. I was near my wit's end with his ass.

"There you go comparing me to a little ass boy who literally grew up with a silver spoon in his mouth. Miss me with the bullshit, Charlie."

"My son wasn't raised with no damn silver spoon!" I interjected, staring at him wildly. I hated when he brought up Jaden.

"But he didn't have to endure nearly as much as me. At least he had you to pick up the slack." Rodney retorted.

I rolled my eyes and bucked aggressively. "Yeah, that's a mother's job. To do what she has to, to make sure her kids are good."

"Exactly! Your son had all of that! I didn't. Between growing up in the projects to a crackhead mother, I'm surprised I'm the only one of my brothers who hasn't done any hard time."

"So, because you didn't go to jail, you deserve brownie points?"

Rodney shook his head and kissed his teeth, his eyes roaming the TV behind me and the floor to ceiling windows.

"I also have a legitimate job and no kids or baby momma drama like most of the niggas I know. I'm literally out here beating generational curses and you're stressing me about leaving the toilet seat up and not taking out the garbage?" He spat defensively.

"I'm so tired of hearing your fucking sob story. Your mother has been clean since you were twenty-one. And you work for fucking Amazon as a regular warehouse associate. Get the fuck out of here with that "breaking generational curses" bullshit."

"Real shit though Charlie," he emphasized, nearly begging me to agree. I hated when he used that whack-ass New York slang on me as if it were the gospel.

"Listen, I don't give a fuck about what you're saying! I am not your fucking maid. I'm already paying most of the bills in this bitch. The least you could do is keep the fucking house clean. How do you think I feel having to come home after a fourteen-hour shift to a dirty house?"

Why the fuck was I still putting up with this nigga, especially when I knew I was the catch? At thirty-four years old, I was fit, feminine, and fine. Standing at five foot seven, I weighed one hundred and sixty pounds and had butterscotch skin as smooth and clear as a baby's butt. While I wasn't the most curvaceous, I had a pretty decent shape with grapefruit-sized breasts and a nice supple ass. My oval shaped angular face sat atop my long, beautiful neck, sporting a sexy collarbone paired with high cheekbones and juicy pouty lips. I wasn't the baddest bitch out there, but my entire package including the fact that I had silky relaxed hair that reached a little past my breasts, kept my nails done, and sported sexy outfits, gave me an edgy sex appeal that couldn't be denied, not even by Stevie Wonder.

Not to mention I worked my way up to the head nurse of the most prestigious hospital in New York City. Nothing was given to me, I worked hard for everything I had. From the time I gave birth to my first and only son at thirteen years old, I didn't get any breaks. Starting as a certified nursing assistant making nine dollars an hour in LaGrange, Georgia, I worked my way to an LPN then flew to New York for a free nursing fellowship and never looked back. I struggled for years as a single mother, and I wasn't blaming my parents like Rodney constantly did. I was sick of his lame ass excuses.

"Look, I work long hours too, doing strenuous hard labor, way harder than you so don't come in here talking all that shit, just because you make more money than me. I'm still your man and the man of this house!" He asserted, getting up from the couch that was full of popcorn kernels. As he stood up several peanuts and M&Ms flew on the floor as well.

"How are you the man of this house and I'm the one paying the rent, the electric, the water, and both of our life insurances? All you pay is the cable bill. Not to mention, last time I checked, my name was the only one listed on the lease for this apartment."

Rodney's nostrils flared; his whole face teetered with aggression. "I don't care how much you make or how many bills you pay, I'm the only one in this bitch with a dick, so therefore I am the man around here," he said, basing up at me. His dark eyes were jumping with rage, while his chiseled chin was locked still. Despite the fear he tried to incite, I wouldn't back down. Rodney was out of his damn mind and getting a little bit too comfortable. This was my shit. He had me fucked up.

Unafraid, I bucked my eyebrows and stepped even closer to him, invading all of his personal space to the point where I felt his hot ass breath on my face. "A real man is a leader. A real man pays the cost to be the motherfucking boss, rather than screaming about his manhood.

You want me to respect you because you have a penis and an XY chromosome? It doesn't work that way. I respect resources. I respect a man who provides. You can't check me in my own shit because you have nothing to check me with," I spat with a menacing scowl. I was raging with anger.

In a hot second, I felt the wind smacked out of me then Rodney ringing the air out of my lungs as he choked me up. I was gasping for oxygen as he slammed me against the wall so hard, I felt the back of my ribs touch each other.

"You stupid fucking bitch, swearing you're so fucking smart like you know the plight of a black man in this country!" He screamed, spit flying from his mouth landing directly in my eye. He lifted me off the floor by the neck, my feet dangling for gravity. I fought back with the little might I had left despite feeling like my circulation was being cut off.

"You see, what you made me do? You see? You just had to keep fucking with a nigga, pushing my buttons, didn't you!"

"Rah, Rah, Rod, Rodney---, pleaseee." I gasped in between breaths, begging him to stop.

"FUCKKKKK!" He growled as he continued suffocating me, my back caving into the wall from his tight hold.

Just when I felt like I was about to give out, I collapsed to the floor, hitting my tush from the hard thump.

"ARRGH" Rodney screamed then punched two big holes into the

wall, causing me to shriek.

On all fours, I crawled away from him struggling to get from out of his reach. After several baby crawls, I felt his heavy boot lunge into my back. "Where the fuck do you think you're going?"

With my palms stretched across the floor, I continued crawling, scraping my knees as he hovered over me. With each squabble I took, I felt a harder kick in my back and then my side. As he continued kicking me, I gulped each time, until I found the might in my spirit and grabbed a hold of his pants and bit him so hard on the ankle, he cried out.

"OUCHHHH! You stupid bitch!" Rodney yelled. Ignoring his bitching, I bit harder and harder until I ripped a piece of his flesh off and spat it out cold. He tumbled down onto the floor, and I straddled on top and threw blow after blow, socking him in the face with the strength of Stone Cold Steve Austin. I then turned towards my left and grabbed the lamp off the end table and cracked him in the head several times until it shattered into pieces, and he had no choice but to surrender.

I was so winded from fighting. I struggled to get up, feeling the side of my ribs burning like acetone being poured onto a disintegrated nail bed. He lied unconsciously on the floor, dismayed and discombobulated. I bent down and placed my index and middle fingers around his neck.

Perfect! He was still breathing, and I didn't kill the nigga.

With no remorse in my heart, I dragged him by the leg through the apartment. The weight of his body tugged at me, but I pressed on. Although, it was a struggle, I used all of my might to get him to the door. Weary and drained, I managed to open the door and kick his heavy ass out. Unsatisfied with the damage I had done, I dragged his motionless body toward the elevator of my apartment building. A minute later, it arrived, and I kicked him into the elevator and sent his ass straight to the lobby.

As soon as the elevator disappeared, I was reminded of pain, as my entire body began to ache, especially my back. Rubbing my neck, I limped towards my apartment door. It had been years since I've had to fight. After leaving my son's father fifteen years ago, I vowed to never let a man put his hands on me again. My momma and Pappy may have slacked on many things, but one thing for sure and two things for certain, I wasn't raised to take any fucking ass beatings. If anything, I was raised to fight back and if Rodney didn't know before, he was well aware now.

2
GIRL POWER

CHARLESTINA "CHARLIE" THOMPSON

RODNEY DIDN'T STOP CALLING OR TEXTING AFTER I kicked his silly ass out. Instead of blocking his number, I put all his calls on do not disturb and I didn't answer any private calls or texts from non-descript numbers. Today was my first day back to work after taking a week off to rest and nurse myself back to health. Luckily, I didn't suffer any fractions or broken bones. I was just sore as a motherfucker and had some red bruises around my neck, which I treated with ice, peppermint oil, and aloe vera. Buying this combination at the store sent surges through my body. Just looking at the products in my bin shook me to the core as flashbacks of me fighting with Jaden's father as a teenager ran through my mind. It had been a long fucking time since I had to fight, and Rodney was trying to take me back there mentally.

All last week, I avoided getting on Facetime with Jaden and opted for audio calls instead. I didn't want my baby to see me like that. He was a firecracker, and it took a lot for me to get Jaden on the straight and narrow, abandon his demon ways, and turn his life around. After spending a few years in a juvenile home due to gang activity, Jaden came home with an exonerated record and enrolled in Penn State University for Computer Science. My boy was about to graduate with honors in May, and he was already offered three positions at three top IT firms in New York City. I couldn't be prouder, so I refused to worry him with my issues. Momma was a big girl. I could handle it.

Looking down at my Fitbit, I noticed that it was lunchtime. I also noticed that I hadn't reached my number of steps for today's midpoints. I glanced around the brightly lit unit that was less busy than usual. While there weren't too many patients on my entire floor this week, it was still another regular day at New York Presbyterian Hospital. The lack of patients didn't stop the exceptionally cold air from bumping through the wing. In fact, it was colder than usually, causing me to pull my cardigan tighter and hug myself. Shivering, I shook my head repeatedly and cursed softly under my breath. Just as I picked up my iPhone from the standing desk and attached my intercom onto my scrubs, I saw one of the new nursing assistants who transitioned in from Clara Barton High School's LPN program scurry in my direction. Her baby face was etched with worrisome dread and her mouth was slightly agape with her tongue pressed to the top of her teeth.

"What's the matter, Karla?"

Innocent looking with rosy, red cheeks and big wandering eyes, she pursed her lips together and began to crack her knuckles nervously. "Rodney's here. He's coming down the hall, any minute now. He has flowers." Her confused scowl turned into a forced smile.

"Thanks. I'm heading to lunch anyway. I sent out a reminder regarding your assignment for the rest of the shift. See you later," I said then walked away. As a supervisor, I could never display weakness in front of my staff. That would be irresponsible of me.

Gripping my phone in my hand, I exhaled deeply and squinched my nose. I'm pretty sure my nostrils were flaring considering how fed up I was. As I trotted past the swinging doors, I caught Rodney bouncing toward me with a fresh cut, a freshly new man weave install, his beard tapered and groomed, and he was dressed in a fitted turtleneck that accentuated his biceps. He flashed me a smile and his teeth were even whiter. It looked like he was using some new fancy toothpaste and probably squeezed in a visit to the hygienist. Whatever it was, he looked damn good as he stood there holding a huge, nicely decorated bouquet. However, I was still done with his ass. Nothing would allow me to forgive him for putting his hands on me.

"Charlie, I've been calling, and texting and I even went by the house. You're never home and you had the locks changed?" He lamented as he shoved the bouquet in my direction. "Look, baby, I am so sorry for what happened between us. Let's start over. I'm taking better care of myself, and I've enrolled in trade school for HVAC like I've been talking about for a while. By next year, I'll be able to pay all of the bills.

Just work with me, baby. I'm trying," Rodney pleaded.

Although he was fine as fuck, reminding me of what I saw in his sorry ass anyway, he reeked of pity. New York niggas were the nicely best dressed bums I'd ever met. They dressed up their dustiness and shopped until they dropped, but they lacked responsibility and leadership. Shit, I was surprised that I even found Rodney because my dating life sucked for years when I first moved here. Rodney was the best pick I attracted. He was attractive, had a job, and wasn't living with his mother like most of the guys in New York I met. Nonetheless, he was renting a room and sharing a bathroom with four strangers which made it impossible for me to sleep over during the beginning of our relationship, which ultimately explained why he moved in with me.

I folded my arms, refusing his advances. "Rodney, this is my workplace. You can't just come in here making a scene. I don't need anybody in my business," I chided squeamishly.

"Bitch, please. You ain't see a scene yet, stop fucking playing with me." Rodney snapped, threw the flowers on the floor, and yanked me closer. His abrasive nature brought me terror and my fight or flight sense rose immediately. I glanced behind him to the security guard down the hall sitting on an office chair behind a podium desk.

"Help!" I yelled, trying to get the attention of the security guard.

Rodney's eyes widened and he covered my mouth with his hand, muffling me from speaking.

"Shut the fuck up." He threatened with rage in his eyes.

I bit his hand, kneed him in the balls, and slapped him across his face. The impact from my hit sounded off down the hall and that's when the security guard got up from his seat and jogged towards us.

"Charlie, c'mon. Don't do this." Rodney begged. His desperation was scaring me. Rodney only put his hands on me once during our three-year relationship and I forgave him. It never happened again until two weeks ago and that was just something I couldn't look past.

As he leaned forward, reaching for me, I jumped back several times, as if leaping from my fate.

"Charlie, are you okay?" A familiar female voice screeched.

I turned around and found my boss Shelly, the Chief Nursing Officer of New York Presbyterian Hospital. Shelly was a pristine, well-put-to-gether black woman who always looked her best. She never had an off day. Seeing her now was a surprise considering that she rarely walked the halls and we only met once a week for our one-on-one meetings. Throughout my seven years at this hospital, Shelly and I grew really close. She was like a mentor to me.

"No, I'm not. Can security please escort him out?" I demanded pointing an accusatory finger at Rodney.

Shelly raised her eyebrows and folded her arms. "Security, please remove this man from our unit and pull his picture from the cameras. Notify all security personnel that he is banned completely from entering and or receiving care from New York Presbyterian Hospital indefinitely." Shelly, wearing a fitted olive green pantsuit and pink pumps asserted.

"You can't do that bitch. It's my right to enter any hospital for care in the entire city, especially if I'm in distress." Rodney argued, as the big and burly security guard yoked him up.

Stepping forward, she tapped her perfect French manicured index finger under Rodney's chin, lifting his eyes to her tall figure. Shelly was already a tall woman but with pumps, she was at least six foot one, a few inches taller than Rodney. "You're in my house, bitch. What I say goes. And unless you got a lawyer present, what I say can't be challenged. Now get the fuck out of my hospital before I have you arrested for assault." She snarled with a threatening scowl. Her intensity even had me on edge.

"Fuck you bitch." Rodney jeered, scanning Shelly up and down. "She can't protect you outside of this hospital, remember that, Charlie." Rodney snickered, taunting me by flinching.

I backed up slowly, disappearing behind Shelly who was not only taller than me but thicker. Shenelle "Shelly" Fox was a Brickhouse and rightfully so, I allowed her to protect me, not because I was physically afraid of Rodney, but because I didn't want to jeopardize my job by flying off the handle. Shielded behind Shelly, I watched the security guard whisked Rodney away.

"Charlie, my office, right now!" Shelly demanded; seriousness riddled all through her tone.

"What's going on between you and Rodney?" Shelly asked me now that we were in the confines of her office. As lavish as can be, within the last two weeks she rearranged it, and brought in new antique furniture. She also added some new ivy green table sculptures to her collection. Shelly was an AKA, a woman of Alpha Kappa Alpha Sorority Inc, a black Greek letter organization. Excellence without excuse was what she called it.

Twiddling my thumbs, I looked down at my hands, avoiding eye contact.

"Is that a bruise or a hickey on your neck?" She inquired, leaning forward, and inspecting my upper body closely. In defense, I closed my cardigan and pulled my eighteen-inch tresses down to cover both sides of my neck.

"We broke up. Things just weren't working out."

"Well, that's a relief. To get rid of dead weight. I've been telling you since I laid eyes on him, I knew you were out of his league. Let's be for real, Charlie. You're under forty, the Director of Nursing at one of the top hospitals in New York City, you're in shape, you're well rounded, well-traveled, and funny. What the hell were you doing with a warehouse worker?" Shelly had always been a little snooty, but she meant well.

I exhaled deeply then squeezed my eyes shut and opened them again quickly. "You're right and that's why I ended it."

"I know I'm right, but just because you ended it, doesn't mean he's done. Like he said, I can't protect you outside of the building. I'm afraid, you may need to get an order of protection."

I huffed and puffed then looked at Shelly's soft eyes. "I'm afraid you're right again."

Shelly was caramel complected with rich copper undertones that highlighted her red freckles around her nose. Her skin glowed like the jar of honey Winnie the Pooh carried around on his voyages; bright and inviting. Every feature on her heart-shaped face was model-esq; from her slender nose, her soft pouty mouth, and hooded eyelids that she always adorned with a striking shimmery eyeshadow, making sure to never overdo it. Although she was visibly stunning, she hid her natural red hair and colored her eyebrows to match her signature chestnut-colored tresses. Appearing as a redhead gave her a fiery sex appeal that was too much for the workplace. I only had the pleasure of seeing her natural hair color a few times when I first started on the job. Outside of her pleasing aesthetic, she carried an air and strength that exuded confidence like no other. It was obvious that she was an it girl and she never had to try hard to make it known.

Suddenly, she got up from her seat and sashayed behind my chair.

Her commanding stride caused her to glide instead of casually walk. Her sweet, regal perfume invaded my nostrils as she hovered over me. Placing her hands on my shoulders, she began to massage me, digging deep into my muscles. With her delicate fingers, she pressed them firmly into my skin and rubbed me continuously. I closed my eyes, almost forgetting where I was at.

"Charlie, you deserve so much better than Rodney. But you have to believe that you deserve better to attract better," Shelly said, her baritone sounding like a lullaby. She continued working my shoulders, loosening up the tension that stood erect.

After a few minutes and me envisioning myself spread out on an island being pampered by two Greek Adonis's, the massage ceased.

"It's been a while since Sean, and I have had you over. Stop by tonight. Trust me, you need it."

3

ENTANGLED

CHARLIE

THIS WAS THE THIRD TIME I HAD BEEN TO SHELLY AND Sean's beautiful estate on West 110th Street. Both times prior were years ago, when I first moved to New York and Shelly invited me over for the holidays. Like the first two times, entering their five-bedroom penthouse condo felt surreal. It smelled divinely rich as touches of cedarwood, jasmine and lime lingered in the air. Moreover, the décor added the extra razzle dazzle on top of the lovely built-in accents that made up the kitchen and the living room. But nothing topped the fully decked out high-rise patio balcony that led out to the roof, overlooking Central Park. It was an immaculate view.

"Hey, girl. Thanks for stopping by. Mojito or Lychee Martini?" Shelly asked as she held two cocktails atop a glass tray.

"Lychee for sure," I bubbled as I grabbed the drink from her.

"My type of girl." Shelly grinned then turned around and allowed me to admire her sculpted back and alluring peacock tattoo that peeked through her nearly backless blouse. Diagonal spaghetti straps ascended from her shoulders to her lower back, adding an extra flair that was uniquely regal and quirky. Exuding an air of equally balanced sexuality and sensuality, she possessed a softness that was to be admired.

As she led me through the condo, I gazed around marveling over the fine artwork on the wall. They were beautifully painted, afro-centric art at its finest. The figures pranced around in stark black paint with no eyes, mouths, or ears. They were faceless yet striking. Just as I almost got lost in the paintings, Shelly's voice buzzed in.

"Leroy Campbell. Sean's favorite painter. These were all custom orders. Sean and him are friends." Shelly bragged.

Impressed, I smiled. "Nice. Elegant. Where is Sean? I haven't seen him since last year's gala."

"Shit, girl, me either." Shelly laughed as she placed the tray onto the Calcutta marble island. "My high-value man is always busy. Busy tending to our very generous donors." Shelly sighed dramatically as she raised her cocktail straw to her mouth and sipped daintily. "God, I love me some him."

"And I love me some you." Sean's gruff voice filled the air, sounding both effervescent and husky. In walked, Sean, a toasted vanilla hue, and equally tall with a solid, yet slender build. Clean cut, and sporting a low tapered fade, Sean was one of the finest ballers I ever had the pleasure of meeting. He exuded calmness, confidence, and power. He stood erect, his posture intact and admirable, and he was well groomed even down to his manicured fingertips. Far from metrosexual, he still maintained a surety of masculinity, in a sweet, non-threatening way.

Wrapping Shelly into a hug, he embraced her from the back and planted kisses all over her neck.

I watched on as Shelly squirmed in his arms and he continued tickling her until she turned around and returned the gesture. This wasn't just any ole kiss. It damn sure wasn't a peck. She held on, taking control, and sucking his lips. He didn't hold back either, sliding his stealthy, engorged, and veiny arms, down her curves, gripping her ass firmly. Watching them didn't make me feel uncomfortable, in fact, my mouth watered. This was one of the finest couples I've ever met, and they weren't around the way fine. They were fit, fine, and wealthy black folks. I was standing in the home of Sean Fox, CEO and Trustee of New York Presbyterian Hospital. He was a second-generation born American, with family roots in the small island of Barbados. His father was a surgeon, and his mother was a nurse. His family came to New York back in the late 1900s and managed to build an enormous fortune by putting their money in the stock exchange. His father was hardworking, financially literate yet humble. He and his family lived modestly in the projects in East Harlem, while he invested properly, became a member of the Board of Trustees of his hospital and passed down the title and one hundred million dollars to Sean. Since he died Sean has been following behind him and since then he's been growing their fortune. First as a doctor, then a surgeon, and now a CEO at only the age of thirty-nine.

Yup, I did my homework.

"Pardon my rudeness and freshness. How have you been Nurse Thompson?"

"Babe, we're off the clock. You can call her Charlestina." Shelly butted in, nudging her husband in the rib.

Sean flicked me the side eye and stiffened his mouth. "Ouu, that's country."

I laughed, showing all of my teeth. "Yes, it is. I'm originally from LaGrange, Georgia. Born and raised as a Georgia Peach. But please don't call me Charlestina. Charlie is just fine, sir."

Sean stepped closer in my direction, wagging his index finger. "How long have you been here? We don't say sir up north. It's a little too dated."

"You meant borderline racist?" I sassed.

Sean nodded his head rapidly, the fade line from his short, tapered beard was crisper than a Lays potato chip. "Just a little bit."

"I guess you're right. Well, I was raised to address a man as sir, especially in his very own residence."

"Cooperative. Respectful. Abiding." Sean winked his eye. "I like that. Well please just call me Sean, Charlie." The innocent seduction in his eyes danced slowly, churning away at my blouse. Suddenly I felt hot.

"Sean, it is," I twittered regaining my composure, hoping that I didn't do too much or offend Shelly. I turned to face her, and she was seated on top of the island with her legs crossed, holding the stem of her champagne glass loosely and smiling flirtatiously back and forth between me and Sean.

"Well, now that we're acquainted, have you ever tried shrooms before?" Shelly asked with no hesitation.

Mouth agape and eyebrows scrunched, I looked at her stunned. "Huh?"

"Don't get all green on me, Charlie. You heard what I said. It's not like it's a narcotic. In fact, it is highly recommended to treat depression and PTSD. Not to mention, it's been used for centuries in ancient civilizations." Shelly explained.

"So, you've done it before?"

"We both have. Don't worry, you'll love them. We have chocolates and Sean makes this really good magic mushroom-infused tea."

"Really?" I'm pretty sure bewilderedness covered my face as I stood against their fridge staring at the both of them.

"Really, girl! You're in need of a spiritual makeover right now. You've finally got that Pookie or Ray-Ray out of your life, now it's time for an awakening." Shelly stressed, her eyes wide and wild as she jumped off the island and grabbed me by the wrist.

I didn't budge at first until my body lost its resistance and glided away with them. "Don't be scared. Trust me, this is going to be the best night of your life."

The sounds of Doja Cat's hit song *So High* mellowed through the dimly lit room, as I stared down into a hot glass of tea. I had already eaten two small cubes of chocolate that were pretty tasty. Now, I was watching the colors from the artwork bounce off the walls. Balls of red, green, black, and orange danced around the living room and spurted out onto Shelly and Sean's faces. I giggled and giggled as I watched them smile profusely and play footsies with their feet on the couch.

"Come here!" Shelly demanded, motioning me over with her finger.

Slowly, I stood, unaware of my body's gravity. All I felt was a surge of euphoria flow through my body, so instead of walking in a straight line, I gyrated, my hips shaking as if I were a belly dancer. I never laughed more in my life or felt this good and in control, yet completely unaware of my powerlessness. But truthfully, I didn't need to relinquish my power against anyone, for it was in my defenselessness, that I came alive.

While my mind was pumping with dopamine and my heart thumping with joy, my mouth opened in wonder as happy tears streamed down my face.

"Babe, look, we have a crier. She's coming alive." Shelly leaped up off the sofa, and an explosive green hue shot out from under her as she stepped closer to me.

"Wowwwwwwww. You're a power ranger!" I gazed at her intently, my eyes feeling like they spread as wide as can be.

As she reached out to touch me, my heart raced faster causing my stomach to flutter and sunbursts of greens, yellows, and oranges invaded my vision. Suddenly I felt myself being pulled, and tugged until I fully gave in. Through my faltered vision, I stared into Shelly's soft eyes as she sat on top of me, running her fingers through my hair and caressing my scalp. With each stroke of her tiny hands, a warmth infused my body. She bent her head down and kissed me, her lips tasting like delicious glitter, filling me up with a weightless, yet hefty emotion. I was incapable of stopping myself from kissing her back, but the rush, the excitement, and how soft her lips were, reassured me even in my discombobulated state; that this was meant to happen and most importantly, I wanted it. Grabbing onto the back of her neck, I kissed her wildly, our tongues swirling and now our bodies contorting as we ended up spawned out on the couch as if we were the last two contestants in a game of Twister. Ravishing each other, we began tugging at one another's clothes until we were naked.

Her body was a true work of art, coloring outside the lines and confines of conventional beauty. Covered under her suits was a slim thickness, a beautifully crafted figure that was built and not bought. She had the body of Meg the Stallion with her lean height complimenting every curve. Yet, still in all of her discipline and perfection, how she wore her love handles in confidence was the most attractive thing about her. Next to her full breasts that naturally sagged.

Lifting her nipple into my mouth, I circled her areola with hunger. She tasted so good. Completely lost in lust, I shifted my eyes to the other couch, not even startled by a naked Sean stroking himself. That was a beautiful sight to see and that's when it all clicked. I was more than lucky to have this power couple all to myself. I suddenly felt control slithering into my veins, and I revved up my passion, grabbing her tighter until I was reminded that control didn't live here.

Shelly hadn't responded good to my fight for power. She flipped me over on the couch so fast and effortlessly that now she was back on top, apparently assuming her rightful position. The warmth of her entire body soothed me. Shortly after a stint of kissing and touching, she dragged me by the hand off the couch. I followed her curves as she led me to the back seductively. I then felt my right arm being lifted and turned around to Sean holding onto my hand, allowing me to lead him. We were now a train and once we got into that room, and knew all passengers were aboard, all mayhem broke loose.

"Come and help me, baby." Shelly purred; her voice nearly drained out of my immediate consciousness. With a low baritone, most of her words were heard through the mouthing of her lips. Without my permission, Sean lifted me off the ground, my legs now wrapped around his neck. I felt alive in the air, as if I could fly. Gyrating my hips around his head was fun, and once he placed his lips on my clit, my body began to surge.

I squirmed back and forth, biting my lip and rubbing my hands on his shoulders. I felt a rattling whistle from between my legs, shortly realizing that Sean was singing as he slurped my insides. Releasing for air, he circled his lips with his tongue while watching me intently.

"Yum." He cooed until I fell onto my back, landing on the bed.

With my head tipping back and my eyes opening and closing, flashes of light and images of both Sean and Shelly on all fours crawled toward me. It wasn't until I was shaking from pleasure and squeezing my thighs shut, while Shelly clung onto me with a mouth full of my pussy that I realized what the fuck was happening. Before I could even catch my breath from the surging orgasm I had, Sean slid his hard dick deep inside me, causing me to see stars and a few substances orbiting around it.

Sucking onto my lips, he hugged me from under, resting his arms on my shoulders as he thrusted in and out of me. I couldn't moan, I couldn't move, I just felt myself falling into a gigantic pool of water, until he collapsed on top of me, and the weight of his body pressed me further into the bed, where the feeling of wetness became more profound.

"Babe, she's not just a crier. Our girl is a squirter." Sean's husky grunt wasn't something he could just turn off, I noticed.

Snickering persisted, bouncing between them both. "I told you," Shelly crooned. I know a squirter when I see one."

4
DIVINE FEMININITY
CHARLIE

I WOKE UP IN A FRANTIC STATE, TO FIND THAT IT WAS after nine o'clock in the morning. Jumping over the ottoman that stood in front of the empty California King bed, I nearly busted my ass. My clothes nor my phone or purse were anywhere to be found, and neither were Shelly and Sean.

Wait. What happened last night?

As confusing thoughts attacked me, I panicked, pacing back and forth, and shaking until I calmed myself down. Forgetting that my shaking most likely came from the urge to release, I trudged into the bathroom and sat on the toilet, now realizing exactly where I was and what happened.

Did I have a threesome with my boss and her husband who's every-body's boss at work? No, I couldn't have. That would just be downright risky and risqué. Besides, I've never, ever been into women sexually so there was no way that what I think happened, actually happened.

Looking down at my naked body, and the fact that my neck, collar-bone, and breasts were covered in hickeys, didn't do much to convince me that I hadn't broken the code of conduct at work and slept with my boss. But it was obvious that I had. Shivering with fear and utter confusion, I slipped out of the bathroom, then exited the room. The quiet bleakness of their home scared me.

Just as I made my way out into the living room, I saw Sean and Shelly cozied up on the couch wearing onesies.

"Sleeping Beauty is finally awake." Shelly purred, looking directly at my nipples. Her stare caused me to cover my naked body with my arms and rock back and forth.

Shelly motioned towards me, while Sean's concerned eyes fanned over both of us.

"Have you showered yet, babe?" Shelly asked.

My eyes widened out of confusion. "I don't think I have time to take a full one, I have to head to work."

"You're off for the next three days. I cleared it with HR, already. Don't worry, it's not coming from your PTO, vacation time or sick days." Shelly smiled, flickering her eyebrow at me.

Taken aback, I shook my head slowly. "Wow, thank you."

Shelly smiled cheekily and said, "Sure you deserve it."

"Shelly, can I talk with you privately?"

That's when her mouth dropped, and her face went numb. "Sean and I don't keep any secrets. Whatever you want to address, can be done right here in the open." She asserted.

Sean was now looking at the TV intently.

"What happened between us last night?" I asked, backing up and covering myself. I was so self-conscious.

"You're standing in the middle of our home fully nude with hickeys all over your body. What do you think happened?" Sean countered.

"Let's get you showered and dressed. I'm going to whip up some brunch and we'll discuss everything over French toast and mimosas. Sounds good?" Shelly teetered between her sultry and professional voice.

What the fuck did I get myself into?

"Sean and I aren't swingers, so you can get that Will Smith, Jada Pinkett, red table talk shit out of your head," Shelly objected.

"So then, who the fuck are you? Excuse my crassness, but what kind of freaky shit are y'all two into?" I asked as I put my fork down and stared into Shelly's eyes.

Shelly pulled her gaze away from me and looked at her husband. He nodded his head and she proceeded to take a swig of her drink before speaking. "If I hadn't met Sean, I'd probably be a full-blown lesbian. I just love women and so does Sean. We haven't had a girlfriend in a while, but now that things are more under control at work for Sean and me, we've been thinking now might be the time to add another woman to our relationship."

"And you think that person should be me?"

These motherfuckers were crazy.

"Shelly, you're my boss and Sean is both of our bosses," I shrilled, my pitch elevated.

"Ok, and…" Sean retorted. "We won't tell, if you don't," he sung with a childish tone that almost made me forget that I was talking to the CEO of the most reputable hospital in New York City.

"You can't be fucking serious. If we continue this entanglement, it will only be a matter of time before folks at the hospital find out." I argued.

"How do you figure?" Shelly raised a forkful of French toast and waved it at me before swallowing it. "We're three consenting adults. What we do in our personal life is nobody's business. I think we're all mature enough to keep our business out of the workplace."

I was convinced that they wouldn't give up, so I figured it was my chance to decline their offer.

"Look, I don't think I'm cut out for this. I have a lot going on at home. I have a son and a career to protect. This isn't me."

Shelly's brows drew closer as her face tightened. "Girl, you don't have shit going on at home. You finally got rid of the dead weight holding you back. Jaden is a grown-ass man in college and about to graduate. I'm your boss and I'm not going to fire you. Besides you're in one of the best unions in the city, it would take a lot for you to be let go. What the hell are you so afraid of?"

Silence fell, scaring me shitless. They were dead serious.

I couldn't believe that she had called me out so effortlessly just to convince me of the truth I was fully aware of.

"I just don't know. I don't feel right about this."

"You weren't saying that last night." Shelly mocked, as a sly grin crept up the corners of her mouth.

"And neither was your body!" Sean added in. "Want to see the video?"

"There's a video!" I exclaimed; my mouth wide open.

"Yeah, don't worry, it's safe with us. A little keepsake. Especially if you decline to be our girlfriend, we'll always have a copy of the memories we made." Shelly interjected.

With my arms folded, I grunted.

"If it matters to you, we'll delete it." Shelly offered, after noticing my disgruntled disposition.

I exhaled deeply while holding the sides of my face.

"Don't. I want to see it first."

"I knew she'd come around," Sean chuckled. "But seriously though, Shelly told me about the bruises and your roughneck boyfriend coming up to the hospital."

"Ok, and…" I was irritated that Shelly would go blabbing my business to her husband.

"You don't deserve that kind of treatment. You're a catch, Charlie. Look at you. You're gorgeous, smart, and you make great money," Sean said sincerely. "Why deal with a sucker named Rodney when you can allow us two to give you the world, all you've ever dreamed of?"

I was growing more and more suspicious. This just seemed too good to be true.

"But why me?"

"Why not you?" Sean opposed. "You're worthy of the love and life we want to give to you and you're more than capable of handling us." He beamed, then winked his eye at me. Scooting back from the table and opening his arms, Sean smirked. "Come to Daddy."

Bug-eyed, I looked at him, then looked at Shelly for approval. These two were kinky as fuck.

"You heard him. Go ahead." Shelly ordered me.

I got up from my seat and shuffled towards Sean who was just as sexy in a childish colorful onesie as he was in a suit. Something magnetic pulled me to him, causing me to plop onto his lap.

Looking over my body, he raised my chin up to eye level then nibbled on my lip. Instantly, my nipples hardened. Sean motioned his hands down to my nipples and fiddled his finger around my Hershey kiss, drowning me with an intoxicating sensation that made my pussy pulsate. Playing with my nipple and kissing me gently sent explosives through my body, even my feet began to tingle.

I let a moan escape my mouth until I noticed Shelly next to us. She pulled my other nipple out and started sucking it. Sensation was coming from everywhere and I couldn't control myself. I was about to cum already.

Damn these two motherfuckers were powerful.

"I- I -I, ohh, I'm about to cum!" I shouted.

"So, cum for Daddy." Sean whispered, in my ear as he circled his trigger finger around my throbbing wet clit. Shelly continued sucking my nipples, now bouncing from breast to breast, intensifying the pleasure. My body began to twitch which made both of them increase the pressure on both my nipples and my clit. I squirmed in Sean's lap, shaking both of my legs, until I couldn't help it anymore.

"FUCKKKKKKKK!" I exploded, as the orgasm settled in, and liquid streamed down my leg.

Sean popped a quick peck on my lips and gently pushed me off him before he smacked my ass. "Go get cleaned up, and head to your spa appointment with Shelly," Sean directed towards me, then shifted his gaze to his wife. "While you're at it, take her for some shopping too, baby. Whatever our lady wants, she gets!" He iterated while grabbing Shelly in closer for a passionate kiss, which lasted at least one full minute. "I'll see ya'll later. I still have some work to do, a few important meetings, nothing too major, though. Enjoy ya'll day ladies."

He sent us off like nothing happened and continued drinking his coffee and skimming his iPad for the latest news in medicine, I assumed.

The steam from the extreme heat of the hot tub added an extra level of relaxation to our spa experience. To think that I was thirty-four making ninety-five thousand dollars a year and had never been to the spa, was kind of crazy. What the fuck had I been doing all my life? Just working and working and taking care of my son. Doing everything I had to, to make sure he had the head-start and support that I didn't.

I raised my arms and sat back, enjoying the hot water massaging my back and soothing my tired feet. I couldn't believe I went from arguing and fighting Rodney to feeling this good after letting his sorry ass go. These last two days have been mind-blowing and revitalizing that I barely even looked at my phone, outside to check in with my son, Jaden. He was set to graduate in a few months, so we talked a little bit more regularly than his earlier years in college. My baby boy was becoming a man.

Just as I opened my eyes, I was met by a naked Shelly descending herself into the jacuzzi with me. We were separated at first, while she enjoyed the chilled jacuzzi and I opted for the hottest one.

"That other one was too cold huh?" I probed her.

With her long tresses tied into a perfect knot bun, she smiled as she glided through the water in my direction. "Yeah, after a while."

"I figured; you'd make your way over here." I watched her every move as she settled right next to me, invading any personal space I thought I had.

"When's the last time you took a day just to pamper yourself?"

I scratched my head then rolled my eyes. "Like this? Never."

"And to think a southern belle like you would be more in tune with her divine femininity. Like they say, it's not where you're from. It's where you're at."

I nodded my head in agreement. "True. Shelly, I really don't know what to make of the last two days but thank you for making me feel good."

Shelly rested her hand on my thigh submerged under the water. "You deserve it."

"You keep saying that I deserve it, but c'mon girl, I'm a Christian. I don't deserve you sharing your husband with me."

"Our husband." She assured me, with true sincerity riddling the creases of her face.

"You can't be serious."

"Do you see Sean? He's tall, handsome, wealthy and has a very high sex drive. I can't take all of him alone, every night. Besides I love women too. Imagine us being sister wives. We'll always have a friend we can trust. A shopping buddy, a travel companion and just someone to do girl things with."

"Respectfully, Shelly you're in a sorority and I'm sure you have tons of friends you can hang out with. You can't bring another woman into your marriage for those frivolous reasons."

"Those aren't frivolous reasons. All the women our ages are wrapped up in their men or their careers. My line sisters don't have time to hang out with me. We meet once a year for our anniversary and maybe Homecoming if we can make it. Everyone is grown with their own lives. Trust me, there are tons of benefits to polyamory, not just for me and Sean, but mainly for you.”

I lulled my eyes into the back of my head then gave a hesitating nod. “How so?”

“I’ve already got my man, and on top of his wonderful attributes, he’s too busy to cheat. Bringing in another woman is my idea and come on, do I really have to lay out all of the benefits?”

“Yes the fuck you do. I’m actually dying of curiosity.” I sassed.

“No disrespect, but there’s piss in the dating pool. Well, at least that’s what women on Instagram and Tik Tok keep saying. Between men not being real providers and opting to go 50/50 on bills, half of the men being gay, incarcerated, or worse transgender, most of the good men are already taken, and the ones left are of high demand because of the overpopulation of women.”

Shelly was making some really good points that I couldn’t argue. And when you can’t beat them, you’ve got to join them.

“And then you have men like Rodney and most of the men I’ve met in New York. They’re fly, attractive and cool to hang around. They just lack leadership and responsibility.”

“Really?” Shelly asked.

“Really. I’m from the south girl. I’m not used to men over thirty still living at their moms’, not having cars, knowing how to fix things on a car or wanting the go half on the bills. My daddy paid all the bills in the house, and he cleaned windows for a living. Even Jaden’s father took care of me financially and we were together as teenagers and the first few years of our twenties. Men up north are just so different." I confessed, allowing myself to release it all. As bad as it sounded, it was true and summed up my entire dating experience in New York so far.

Shelly nodded her head and continued stroking my leg. "I'm listening girl and that sounds awful."

"Yeah, you really lucked up with Sean. You guys are like the perfect black power couple. I didn't even know black men were CEOs of hospitals."

"They generally aren't but Sean, he's different, so you better be thankful I'm willing to share him with you."

Pressing my fingers to my smiling lips, I nodded slowly, pretty sure my eyes were glowing as I said, "I truly am, although I'm still in awe."

"Save the sentiment for after our shopping spree. I've got my three favorite stylists at my three favorite stores already lined up. Your dressing room at each one is already filled with cute looks I pulled for you. Shoes, bags, and all." She winked. "Now let's hurry up and get there."

5

ROLEPLAY

CHARLIE

"**M**A, WHERE YOU BEEN? I'VE BEEN CALLING YOU for the last few days and haven't gotten any answer. What's up? Everything good with you and that nigga Rodney?" Jaden pried, after I finally answered his FaceTime call.

I forgot that I hadn't filled Jaden in on me and Rodney's break-up. Shit, I forgot about most of my responsibilities outside of work, this last week. Between the mind-blowing sex, dates, and excursions, Shelly and Sean had me on cloud nine. Since I've been at their place this past week, I hadn't even checked my mail, let alone checked my phone. I couldn't keep hiding the breakup with Rodney from Jaden. I figured spilling the beans about our split would ensure I avoided telling him about my new entanglement of a relationship.

"Hey baby. I'm sorry I've been out of reach. Rodney and I broke up maybe two weeks ago." I confessed.

Jaden sucked his teeth. "Two weeks ago? And you're just telling me? Why? What happened."

I huffed and puffed, shaking my head at my concerned son. One thing for sure, he loved his Momma.

"Don't tell me that nigga put his hands on you." He jumped the gun but ironically was spot on.

"No- no- noth- nothing like that." I stuttered.

"Ma, stop lying. You've never been good at it. Just tell me the truth."

I went into my text messages, so the video would pause, and Jaden wouldn't be able to see my face. He knew his Momma. I was a terrible liar.

"Put your camera back on and look at me!" Jaden demanded, his voice elevating up a few pitches.

I did as he said.

"Now tell me the truth. Did Rodney bitch ass put his hands on you?"

Without saying a word, I shook my head no. I had to lie because the fire in Jaden's eyes continued to rise, and he was starting to scare me. Leaning his chocolate face closer to the screen he eyed me suspiciously.

"Oh hell no. This nigga leaving bruises. Ma, I'm telling you when I see that nigga, I'm gon kill him." Jaden hissed; his upper lip curved giving him a menacing look.

"No, no baby. Please, just leave it alone. I kicked his ass out and we're done. Just let it be."

"Let it be? Nah, fuck that. You're my mother and his bitch ass putting his hands on you because he knows I'm not there to protect you. Ain't nothing you can say that'll make me let this shit slide. His ass will be dealt with. Believe that." Jaden scowled.

I bit my lip, searching my mind for what to say. With everything in me, I lowered my tone. I needed Jaden to hear how serious I was.

"Listen to me carefully, Jaden. As your mother, who is a grown-ass woman, I am telling you to leave it alone. You're about to graduate and start your career. You have your whole life ahead of you. I do not want you throwing it away to protect me. I am your mother. It's my job to protect you, so believe me when I say, me and Rodney are done!"

Jaden's nostrils were flaring while his shoulder length dreadlocks bounced across his face as he shook his head repeatedly. "Ma, I hear you. But I ain't listening."

"And that's always been your problem, not listening boy." I cracked a giggle to lighten the mood.

He didn't budge.

"How's everything going with you babe? You ready to see your graduation pictures?"

Silence, accompanied by an unimpressed frown painted his face.

"I gotta go, Ma. I'ma talk to you later," he said quickly and ended the call, leaving a black screen staring back at me.

Today was already off to a bad start and it was only two o'clock in the afternoon. I slid out of the empty break room and made my way back toward the unit. I started my shift four hours ago and had another ten hours to go. My talk with Jaden was my true wake-up call. Paradise was over. I had to return home today and face my reality and tend to my house. I was a newly single woman and Jaden was set to come back home in four months. All of the job offers he received were in New York, so regardless to which one he chose, I had to make room for my baby until he got his own place. That meant turning Rodney's old game room around.

Outside of that, I just needed to get my head together, so I pulled up my messages and shot Shelly a text.

Heading home tonight. Got some stuff to tend to.

Immediately, her text receipts appeared as read. She liked my message shortly after without replying back. Somehow through the phone, I could sense her uneasiness.

The rest of my shift seemed to go by so fast because I was actually busy with my staff and administering a treatment plan for two clients. The more I limited using my phone at work, the quicker my grueling fourteen-hour shift went by. Nonetheless, when I finally took my break and retrieved my phone from my bag, I noticed seventy missed calls and fourteen text messages from Rodney. This was the most he had called since the breakup. The fact that I ceased all communication with him had him going crazy. I hadn't responded to one text or answered one call from him. The last time I saw him was when he came up to the hospital unannounced, and since then I've been locked in Neverland with Sean and Shelly and haven't been home.

Seventy missed calls were a tad bit excessive. Putting him on DND wasn't enough. Looking down at the screen, my hands trembling, I knew it was time to get a new phone number. I couldn't move on with my past constantly trying to get a hold of me. As I closed all the apps on my phone, a text message from an unsaved number popped up.

Meet me on the twentieth floor, NOW!

Shelly just wouldn't quit and now she was bringing it to work which made me uneasy. The last thing I needed were colleagues in my business. Just as I was texting her back, another message came through.

Save the chatter. I make the demands and I ask the questions. Get up here NOW!

I looked down at my phone appalled but slightly turned on. This woman was good looking and bossy. Having never been with a woman before, her sass turned me on just how the charm of a man would. It was weird, but I was growing an attraction to Shelly that I hadn't expected. So, I erased my message and made my way toward the elevators. Walking swiftly, hoping to avoid any of my nursing staff from inquiring about my whereabouts or even spotting me dipping off.

While waiting for the elevators, I twiddled my fingers nervously. I didn't know what to expect, but I was hoping that Shelly didn't do the unthinkable, or perhaps the unspeakable.

We were in a place of business, for Christ Sakes.

Now in the elevator, I tapped my foot several times, not knowing what to expect when those doors finally opened. Staring at the monitor that displayed the progression of the floor numbers as we ascended up,

I exhaled in and out and rolled my shoulders back several times. Anxious was an understatement. As the elevator dinged and signaled that we had finally made it to the twentieth floor, the doors slid open and to my surprise; standing in front of me was Sean with his tie unloosened and suit jacket nowhere to be found. His rich burnt vanilla-colored skin produced a threatening spontaneity, that I never experienced, as I was not normally attracted to light skinned men. Nonetheless, I couldn't deny that Sean was fine as fuck.

Curling his index finger, he beckoned me off the elevator. The lights on the entire floor were dim, considering that this was one of the floors that we didn't use for patients; only meetings and to store loads of drugs. Only the Director of Nursing, myself, Shelly, and Sean had free access to this floor. RNs could come to this floor to retrieve drugs, but they needed signed approval from me before they came up.

I followed Sean's tempting eyes, as he never turned around to lead me. Instead, he lured me with inviting irises and an enticing smirk on his lips. I stepped inside the examination room, and he closed the door. On the sink sat several trinkets: handcuffs, a whip, lube, strawberries, and whip cream.

Once the door was closed, instantaneously, Sean grabbed me and spread my body out on the table. Shivering from his intensity as he peeled my scrubs off, I stared into his eyes. My trust deepened each moment I looked at him. He didn't even have to say a word, I knew that I could count on him to protect me. His stature, his sense of sincerity, and his title made me feel like a kept woman, whose best interests he always had at heart. Whatever he asked me to do, I felt compelled to as if I was under some type of spell. The way he carried himself just made me naturally want to submit to another woman's husband. Life was truly fucking crazy. I never thought I'd ever be the other woman. I vowed to never deal with a married man in my past and yet here I was.

Now completely naked on the table, Sean licked every crevice of my body. First starting to swirl his tongue on my breasts, he motioned his lips up to my lips and we kissed passionately as his hands wandered from my breasts to my belly button then my thighs. When we kissed, it felt like I was kissing my man of umpteenth years, that I had built this sexual chemistry with. But Lord was that further from the truth.

As he nibbled on my lips and played with my clit, slowly strumming it with his trigger finger, my eyes rolled into the back of my head. He then brought his tongue down to my nipples circling my areola repeatedly, adding another level of sensation.

"Ouu, ouu," I moaned, and he covered my mouth with his palm. I began licking the inside of his hand, tasting the million-dollar sweat that represented how hard he worked.

Damn, he tasted good.

He now inserted his middle finger inside of me. The sound of my gushy pussy being finger fucked added not only to my excitement but intensified my pleasure. I normally didn't like to be finger-popped, but everything with Sean felt just right. He was turning me out in an innocent way, helping me to revive my sexuality by making me revisit my childhood sexual experiences, and now that I was an adult, I could truly enjoy it. He was making me feel good in ways Rodney never even scratched the surface.

As I stared into his eyes, holding on for dear life, a mischievous smile appeared on his face. Fidgeting, he reached over to his suit jacket while continuing to rub his thumb against my clit. Moments later his sinister grin returned as the persistent sound of a strong vibration alarmed me. My body clenched up as the vibration became louder until I wasn't able to ignore the sound or the feeling. Sean raised the small blue bullet for me to see and chuckled. He then slid his mouth down to my pussy and spat viciously before going in for the kill. He slurped, he sucked, and lapped up my juices, then raised the bullet onto my clit.

It felt so good, my legs started shaking and my body started contorting as the vibration intensified. As he strummed my pussy, tracing the clit up and down with the bullet, I covered my mouth, hoping to quiet myself down. I could feel the big O coming.

Sean didn't care. He scurried out of his pants and in the matter of a second, he was deep inside of me. I didn't even get to see whether or not he put a condom on and from the way it felt, I'm pretty sure he didn't.

"You got some good pussy on you, Charlie," he grunted as he pumped inside of me, causing the exam table to rock back and forth.

His thrusts sped up as his dick became harder and harder inside of me. Looking down at me, trying to hide the pleasure on his face, he choked me. His grip around my neck was so tight, I felt my vision becoming cloudy. Then his thrusts became harder and harder until a warm liquid invaded my canal and he fell flat on top of me, panting.

"I'm sorry but I haven't had no pussy like that in years. Fuck", he said as he lifted off of me and kissed me.

The fear I had earlier turned into damn right panic as I thought about the fact that this married man ejaculated in me. As we lay there on the exam table, I felt his heartbeat slow down, but mine was pumping hard. As I heard footsteps approach the door, my heart began pumping louder.

Tossing and turning, I tried kicking Sean off, but he wouldn't budge. His hold on me just became stronger.

"Relax," he said forcefully yet low and intense.

The sensation was stopping me from warning him of our guest. Seconds later, Shelly walked in wearing a long white coat. The click-clack of her heels drowned out the sound of the vibration, along with the sensation. I was shivering inside as she approached the head of the examination table. She didn't once look at Sean and he never stopped applying pressure on my clit.

Now standing in front of me, she slid off her white coat revealing a short, sexy cosplay nurse outfit. The short tennis skirt showed a peek of her round, supple ass. Shelly smacked her red kissable lips, which made an intoxicating smooching sound.

"Who told you to start without me?" Shelly demanded answers, her voice stern and stony.

That's when Sean raised off the exam table, his dick wet and erect. He stood up facing Shelly. With sweet ecstasy on my face mixed with a hint of embarrassment, I leaned up on the examination table. Staring at the married couple while they stared at each other was an intense exchange. Without saying a word, Sean stepped closer to Shelly and grabbed her by the neck. At first, his gesture looked playful, until the wrenching sound of his grip tightening around her neck ripped through the room.

"Stop, Sean. You're hurting her!" I raised my voice, as I rushed toward them, latching onto Sean's arm to tug him away. Watching him handle his wife like that brought back the terror of him choking me just a few minutes ago. It's interesting how watching a violent act could cause more trauma than actually experiencing it.

Sean smacked my arms, which pushed me away. I didn't dare challenge him.

"Who told you to question me?" Sean said to Shelly.

"Nobody Daddy."

"Good, now open up!" He instructed.

Shelly did as she was told and opened her mouth wide. Sean snorted loudly and hog spit directly into her mouth. My eyes widened as I watched this disgusting exchange. The wildest thing was the lustful smile dancing on Shelly's face. She closed her mouth and then licked her lips.

"Yummy!"

"Assume your rightful position," Sean instructed as he let go of her neck.

Shelly immediately dropped down to her knees and stuck her tongue out. This time I was in a clear state of mind and able to see it fully. The first night when I was on shrooms, everything was magnified. Everything felt good. However, Sean lived up to the hype even while I was sober. His penis was to be worshipped. Long, meaty, and full of girth, it was the prettiest dick I'd ever seen. Although he was high yellow, the sun sure didn't shine down there. The color of his dick was as chocolate as me. With a head so round, big, and clean, I almost forgot that I was looking at a penis. For some reason I thought that I was at a museum examining an art exhibit. Lord he was strapped beautifully.

Nonetheless, he was nothing short of violent. For him to have such a magnificent penis, he toted it like a weapon as he shoved it forcefully down Shelly's throat, damn near making her choke. I watched on as he fucked her face viciously, not giving her any mercy. Shelly took it like a champ. In fact, she looked like she enjoyed every moment of it considering how hard her nipples poked through her costume. Not to mention, the ecstasy on her face and the moaning she disguised as gagging told me all I needed to know. These two were into roleplaying and rough sex.

I couldn't help but join in as my pussy started to throb from the intoxicating sounds Shelly made as she gagged on her husband's dick. My nipples hardened and my pussy got wetter, so I slowly backed up and laid on the table. Legs cocked open as wide as a canal; I strummed my clit along to the steamy sight in front of me. With sticky semen painted on the inside of my thighs, I knew I'd have to clean up well after this. However, at this moment, I didn't have to try hard to relax and enjoy the moment.

"Swallow it all for Daddy, you nasty slut," Sean spat as he fucked her throat holding back nothing.

His forcefulness excited me more and now my clit was throbbing so much, it began to pulsate.

Sean pulled his dick out of Shelly's mouth and slapped her hard in the face with his hand. The impact from his slap sent chills through my body. Shelly's eyes were wet as her eyeliner created a puffiness under her eyes. Despite how tired and worn out she looked, the eagerness to please her man never left, it only intensified.

Grunts rolled out of Sean's mouth as he continued thrusting in and out of Shelly's wet hole. He didn't bother to moan, he just kept the same motion, allowing minute utters to signal the pleasure he was re-ceiving. That wasn't until I saw his ankles shake.

"Arrgh, fuck," he belted out as he shoved his dick deeper down her throat, holding onto her shoulders tightly.

He exhaled deeply, as I watched the tension roll down his shoulders, to his legs and completely out of his body.

Shelly, still on all fours licked her lips, tracing her tongue around her entire mouth. "Yum."

"Get ready for the big one," Sean instructed as he jacked his dick savagely until semen came dripping out, which he plastered right onto Shelly's face. Something about how rough he was in contrast with how he appeared as a gentle giant turned me on. I plucked at my clit swiftly until I let out a loud "ahh". By time I opened my eyes, Shelly was up from her knees wiping her face off with a paper towel and Sean was fixing his pants. What a wonderful work break!

As I sat back watching the married couple act like nothing had just happened, Sean walked over to the sink area and opened one of the cabinets. He pulled out two jewelry boxes. Both were velvet yet different colors and sizes. He turned to face me and said, "I'd hate to forget this because you've earned it," he said as he shoved the boxes in my face.

Reluctantly, I grabbed, them as I watched Shelly out the corner of my eye with a warmhearted smile on her face. As I opened the large rectangular box, a diamond necklace set blinged in front of me.

"It's a diamond chevron eternity necklace, fourteen karat, white gold," Sean boasted.

My heart skipped a beat as I gasped aloud.

"No, you're not dreaming, babe. It's our gift to you. We know you've been through a lot these last few weeks. We just want to show you how much we appreciate you." Shelly interjected.

My head was spinning, and my heart was beating fast as I sat there on the exam table with a loss for words.

"That's not even the best part. Open the other box." Sean added.

Fidgeting, I closed the first box then opened the smaller one. Staring back at me was the most beautiful ring I had ever seen. It wasn't big enough to be a wedding ring but nonetheless still beautiful.

"Wh-wh-what is this?" I asked, dumbfoundedly.

"It's an engagement ring. Will you be our girlfriend, Charlie?" Shelly asked.

For a second, I felt like I was about to collapse. I could not believe my ears.

"Yes, you heard right. We want you to be our girlfriend. You don't have to decide now. You can take your time to think about it and still keep the necklace. When you're ready to make the commitment to us, then you can have the engagement ring." Shelly explained.

I looked back and forth at both of them, completely flabbergasted and at a loss for words.

6

PROPERTY

CHARLIE

Two Weeks Later

"**B***ITCH YOU WILL NOT BELIEVE WHAT THE FUCK* I've got myself into!" I exclaimed as I looked across the table at Sade. We were at Soco, our favorite brunch spot in Clinton Hill. Sade and I met a few years back at Methodist Hospital. We both started our careers in the nursing fellowship I moved to New York for and have been tight ever since. Although I felt like I was too old to make new friends when I moved here, the truth was that Sade was my best friend.

"Shit, yes I will. Since you've broken up with Rodney, your ass has been MIA. Missing in motherfucking action. What's the word, sis?" Sade was a Brooklyn girl for real, from the gold rings covering her fingers to her old school flat twist hairstyle and the gold tooth in her mouth. Looking at Sade, you would have thought it was 1993 and not 2023. Nonetheless, her caramel complected skin was flawless without a blemish in sight and she had beautiful features such as her full lips and bright smile.

Looking into her Chinese-slanted eyes, I picked up my hands that I kept hidden on my lap and placed them on the table. "Boom!" I announced as I shoved my ring finger in her face.

Sade's brows narrowed together as her eyes scanned my finger up and down. "Rodney's ass proposed girl?"

I leaned forward, hovering over my salad. "Fuck no!" I whispered.

Sade followed suit, mocking me as she leaned forward as well. "So, who proposed?" The satire in her response was loud despite how silent her whisper was.

That's when I sat up in the chair and looked at her gravely.

"You remember my boss, Shelly?"

"Yeah, she's married to that fine ass man. Isn't he the CEO of Presbyterian?"

I nodded my head slowly and watched Sade's eyes widen as she picked up her glass of water. She took a long sip before placing it back on the table.

"Wait, so let me get this clear? Your married boss, who's a woman proposed to you?"

Pursing my lips, I nodded my head slowly again.

"When the fuck have you been into girls?" She interrogated me.

"Never!"

"So, what the fuck are you talking about? Come on girl, stop playing with me!"

"I'm not playing with you. I'm in a polyamorous relationship with

Shelly and her husband Sean!" I revealed.

Sade's nostrils flared as she took a deep breath and then exhaled shortly after. "Bitch, what! You've got to be joking!"

Bouncing my eyebrows once, I looked at Sade with a flat expression. Sade's eyes widened as she covered her mouth.

"Bitch, please share all of the details. NOW! How long has this been going on?"

I reached over the table and tugged at her arm. "Hush!" I warned as I held my index finger to my mouth. "Don't talk too loud."

"All right bitch, just spill it already."

"Okay, so shortly after I broke up with Rodney, he wouldn't stop calling me."

Sade rolled her eyes and shook her head obnoxiously. "Yeah," she egged me on.

"So, after not answering his calls for a few weeks, he decides to come to the hospital and shows his ass."

Sade twisted her lip giving me the stink eye. "Typical Rodney shit!"

"Yeah, so Shelly pops up out of nowhere and checks his ass. She even had security escort him out. After that she invited me to her office. She starts telling me that I deserve better than Rodney and how much of a catch I am."

Sade was completely invested in the story, hanging onto every word I said as she mouthed the words that I spoke.

"Then she invited me to her house. So, I get there, and she and Sean are eating magic mushroom-infused chocolate. They gave me one and the rest of the night was a blur. I do know that I came at least three times though."

Sade's mouth dropped open as she yanked me by the arm.

"What! Nah, that's crazyyyyyyyyy!"

"What's even crazier is how they gave me this engagement ring and asked me to be their girlfriend. They also gave me a diamond necklace."

"Dayummmmmmm girl! Meanwhile, I just need my rent paid for a few months. Please teach me!" She hollered, catching the attention of several parties seated near us.

"Girl, when I tell you I did not plan this. I had no idea that one visit to their house would turn my life around. I haven't been home in a month."

"Thank God you don't have any pets or little kids. ACS and Animal Patrol would have been on your ass." Sade cackled.

"I may not have any little kids, but I still have a son who's coming back home in a few months. How the hell am I going to explain that I went from an ain't shit nigga to a poly relationship? There's no way my grown son is going to respect that."

Sade shrugged and bit her lip. "Fuck it. You don't have to tell him."

I scratched my head, actually contemplating Sade's silly suggestion. "I don't have to tell him, but how long can I really keep it a secret? I'm already ducking his Facetimes and dodging his calls. I had to confess about Rodney and me breaking up and now he knows about the abuse."

Sade covered my hand with hers and rubbed it gently. "I know babe, but now that that's over, it's time for you to get used to being treated like a Queen. Shelly and Sean are balling. Being their girlfriend will only benefit you."

I exhaled slowly and sat up straight, prepared to hear Sade make sense of this absurd reality.

"Look, I know this is risqué, but Shelly and Sean have too much to lose for this to get out of hand. Just look at it as the blessing it is. If they're already cashing out on expensive jewelry, and the sex is good, imagine what else will come with this arrangement. I'm thinking shopping sprees and traveling overseas."

"They already took me on a lavish shopping spree at Louis Vuitton and Chanel. I have so many bags, shoes, and clothes, I don't know what to do with them. You know I'm still a country girl at heart. I've never been into the flashy stuff. I leave that for you New Yorkers." I added.

Sade smiled boldly, showing both sets of teeth. "Now it's your time to shine baby. And you've got not only one but two people ready to spoil you and make your life comfortable. Enjoy it. Imagine what this can also do for your career!" Sade gleamed.

I sat back in my seat and allowed myself to dream, something I hadn't done since I was a little girl. Images of me laid out on a private island, getting a massage invaded my mind. A beautiful sunset sat behind me as Sean fed me grapes and Shelly massaged my feet. I did deserve to be treated like a queen especially after raising my son alone all of these years, working hard, long, sweat-filled hours and putting up with Rodney's trifling ass.

I exhaled deeply, my paradise vision fading away and looked at Sade. "I guess you're right girl. Being with them won't hurt me, especially not more than all the pain I've already endured."

After damn near pleading with the Fox's to spend a night away from them, I jumped in an Uber and made my way across the Williamsburg Bridge to my apartment building on the Lower East Side of Manhattan. Luckily there was no traffic, so the usual forty-minute drive really turned out to be half of that. As the Uber driver slowed down in front of my building, I hesitated to get out once I noticed a family of rats near the corner store.

"Good night!" The Asian male said.

"Just wait a minute. You see those big ass rats over there?"

The Asian man chuckled and turned around to face me. "It's New York, rats run the city. Please hurry. I have to pick up my next ride," he dismissed me abruptly.

I sucked my teeth in disgust not because what he said wasn't true, but because he showed no concern. All he cared about was money. Like everyone else in New York, he was chasing a dollar, but lacking common courtesy for his neighbor, let alone customer. I took a deep breath and unlocked the door and stepped out. For early February, the weather wasn't too bad. Global warming surely changed things. My first few winters up here were brutal. New York in the winter was nothing like the month and a half of coldness I grew up experiencing in Lagrange, Georgia.

I scurried to the front door of my building holding my bag tight and securing myself from any muggers. After my first time getting robbed in New York years ago, I stayed on alert, ensuring that it never happened again. Just as I tapped my keycard on the intercom and the door opened, I was startled by Rodney who jumped up from one of the lazy chaises situated in the lobby of my building. His beard was scruffy, signaling that he definitely was due for a haircut. All in all, he had me on edge just from his wild eyes and sketchy movements.

"There's my fiancée' right there," he announced, looking back and forth between me and the security guard who sat behind the elaborate desk plastered in the middle of the walkway.

Hesitantly, I gripped my bag even tighter and slowly paced forward.

"Miss, do you know this man?" The young black male security guard asked.

As I looked around the lobby, I noticed that it was moderately full of residents getting off the elevators, walking back and forth towards the gym and or mailroom. There were even a few seated in the lobby reading a newspaper or typing away on their laptop. My apartment building was one of the most expensive in the area. Although I got this apartment through Housing Connect, I still paid the most considering that my income was on the latter end of the threshold. Everything was new including our gym, pool, and café areas. Not to mention I was one of the only five black tenants in the building. The last thing I wanted to do was create a scene, especially since another security guard let me off the hook for the fight that Rodney and I had a month ago. So, I shook my head and obliged.

"Yes sir. I do."

"Okay, great. Let me have your ID?" The security guard requested, looking at Rodney. Rodney inched forward and provided his ID quickly. As I watched him, my temperature started to rise, and I became hot. My palms were sweating, and my neck twitched a few times. I just didn't feel good about seeing Rodney and I was hoping that I had the gift of gab to get him to leave me alone.

After he signed his name and the security guard issued him a visitor's pass, I walked past Rodney swiftly, hoping to dodge him. Without running or jogging, his long legs allowed him to not miss a beat. As I made my way towards the elevators, Rodney was on my ass. I was hoping to catch the first elevator that was full of people, but it closed suddenly which meant that Rodney and I were going to be alone in this elevator.

I rocked back and forth watching the elevator decline from the sixteenth floor all the way toward the lobby. Rodney never once said a word, but his cologne and his dampening spirit spoke loudly. Once on the ground level, the elevator doors slid open, and a couple stepped off and walked around us. Rodney stepped inside first, and I followed behind him.

The doors closed and the elevator shot up. I expected Rodney to speak but he still remained quiet, which made me even more nervous. I had no idea what he was plotting but I could feel him staring a hole into my back. His negative energy was so strong, the elevator reeked of gloom. As the elevator crept up to the ninth floor and the door opened, I scurried out quickly, nearly running towards my apartment door. As I fumbled in my bag for my keys, I dropped them right out of my hand and Rodney picked them up.

"Step aside. I got it boo," he asserted.

My knees were shaking, and I was damn near trembling as I watched him enter the key inside the keyhole and turn the lock. Once the door opened, he stepped inside. I hesitated to enter, and at the sign of my reluctance, he yanked me by the wrist pulling me into the apartment and shutting and locking the door.

Immediately once inside, he slammed me against the wall.

"I told your fucking ass you can't hide from me if you tried. Now it's been a month and you haven't been home, so who's the new nigga?" He screamed.

I tasted the salt from my tears as they streamed down my face to my mouth as I stared at him.

"BITCH, YOU HEAR ME TALKING TO YOU! ANSWER ME!" Rodney spat, spit flying in my face.

I shook my head no slowly. I was so petrified; I couldn't even speak.

"Now your dumb ass is loss for words huh? But you had all that mouth at the hospital, right? I told you that bitch couldn't protect you outside of those walls."

I tried to slide away but Rodney grabbed me by the neck and pinned me on the wall, raising me up from the floor, just as he did last time.

"Now I'm going to ask your stupid ass one more time. Who the hell have you been fucking?"

"N-n-n-no-nobody." I managed to get out, although I was short of breath.

Whack.

Rodney punched me in my face so hard, it felt like my eye popped out of the socket. "Stop fucking lying," he argued as he loosened his grip on my neck and I slid down the wall, planting my feet on the ground.

I was thankful because I thought that after he punched me, it was over. I hadn't expected things to get worse, until he picked up my hand.

Nostrils flaring, his face flushed with fire in his eyes, he raised my hand to eye level and yelled, "What the fuck is this, Charlie?"

I shook my hand away, determined to hide it.

"So, you're engaged? That fast? So, you just said fuck me and fuck us? Fuck what we have?"

Tears continued to flow from my eyes, as I struggled to find the words to say. But it was too late, Rodney's hands started flying and he landed punches all over my face. As he choked me again, trying to squeeze the life out of me, I bit him hard on the forearm and kneed him in his balls. That got him off me and I ran through the house frantically, in search of my phone, then realized it was in my bag which was near Rodney. There was no way I could go back over there so I kept running through the living room, until I felt Rodney grab me by my hair. His fingers were latched around my tresses so tightly that I felt my scalp being lifted from my head, as I tried to run away.

Nonetheless, I couldn't so Rodney dragged me by the hair, towards the back of the house.

"You think you can do better than me? You think I'm just gon let you give away my pussy like that? Bitch you're out of your mind!" He yelled as he pulled me into the bedroom I once shared with him. Once inside he threw me across the room, and I hit the hardwood floors, scraping my elbow.

Rodney slammed the door and locked it and that's when doom settled in. He turned around and tore his belt off. "Ain't nobody getting that pussy if I can't. That's my pussy bitch!" He raged sinisterly.

Unable to get up, I scurried back, sliding across the floor as Rodney stepped closer and closer in my direction. I had finally hit the wall of the windowsill and there was nowhere else to go. Rodney's corner lip raised as he tightened his jaw, looking over me with pure hatred in his eyes.

He reached down and grabbed me up by my collar. Now standing face to face with him, he swallowed my lips anxiously as if he was trying to suck my face off. He continued kissing me, and grabbing my ass, as he motioned me towards the bed we once shared. He then forced me down, his heavy body trapping me under his. As he squandered on top of me, I felt his penis harden and that's when more tears came down my eyes. I knew that there was nothing I could do to prevent what was about to happen.

"Stop all the fucking crying. You've fucked me plenty of times before, don't act like you too good to take this dick now!" He barked.

As he hovered over me with no care in the world that I was distraught, he ripped open my pants and pulled them down. He then lowered himself onto me as he squirmed out of his pants. Part of me wanted to fight back but I was terrified of what he would do so I laid still until I felt him force his way inside of me. Nothing about it was pleasurable, for me that was.

I laid there like a doormat allowing him to pump in and out as I closed my eyes until I felt a slap on my face.

"Look at me!" He screamed.

My eyes shot open as tears rolled down my cheeks.

"Umph. Umph. This pussy wet as fuck!" He grunted.

Just the sound of his grunts tore me up inside. He didn't care, he just kept pounding away and moaning and grunting and enjoying himself while I lied under him utterly broken from degradation. It seemed like it took him forever to finish, but when he did, he didn't bother to pull out. Instead, I felt his slimy liquid slither inside me. Making sure I got every ounce of it, he pushed deeper inside of me, causing me to yell out from the pain.

"Shut the fuck up and take that dick. It's over anyway. I already came," he said, as if I didn't already know.

Before he got up from the bed, he kissed me on the forehead, then grabbed my hand and ripped my engagement ring off.

"Don't worry, I'll get you a better one soon, because you belong to me!"

7

TRASH

CHARLIE

DAY 1

BEFORE RODNEY LEFT, HE TORE MY ROOM UPSIDE down. I laid on the bed broken, watching him pull out drawers and toss my clothes everywhere. He searched through my bag and came across the diamond necklace, which made him search through my closet. Luckily all the stuff Shelly bought me on our shopping spree was at their house. At least I had something left from the Fox's and I didn't have to endure another ass beating or sexual assault because of Rodney's anger. Instead, when he didn't find anything else, he took the ring and necklace and said that he'd be back in a day or two with his stuff.

I knew that meant he was most likely about to pawn the diamonds and who knew if he'd be back. Truthfully, I had no reason to panic. He already took the best of me so what was left to fear? Instead of running and hiding, I continued to lay in the same spot he left me, allowing hours and hours to pass without even getting up. When I could no lon-

73

ger hold in my urine, I allowed my bladder to release. Warm liquid saturated the sheets and penetrated the mattress where I laid, until I had done it again and again.

I couldn't believe that I was violated again by someone that I trusted. And to think that I shared my past with Rodney for him to turn around and do the same thing? To strip me of my power and voice? To leave me feeling even weaker than I had ever felt. It had been years since I revisited the sexual trauma of my past, and Rodney made it all resurface and as much as I tried to move, I was crippled.

So crippled to the point that I ignored the loud growling that belted from my stomach. Seeing as I didn't eat anything, the urge to defecate never came, which I was truly grateful for because I don't know if I would have been able to make it to the toilet. Thank God I didn't have to face that because the level of depression I was feeling could have very well resulted in me shitting on myself.

I stared out the window watching the faint sunrise turn into a gloomy overcast of clouds that blocked out any sunlight. Twiddling my thumbs, I watched a peek of sunlight come out a few hours later, until the sunset again and that's when I knew the workday had passed. I didn't bother to call out. In fact, there was no way to make a call anyway after Rodney broke my phone. Next to the whirlwind of clothes on the floor was my phone shattered in pieces. Rodney made sure to leave me and everything I owned broken and beyond repair.

It would take more than therapy to get over this. There wasn't enough time in the world for me to heal because I felt like there was no fixing me. I just had to accept my past and my destiny. Like so many other black women, I had been violated as a young girl and just when I thought the cycle of trauma was waning, it had been reignited.

As a thirty-four-year-old woman, I truly had no idea if I'd be able to recover. But only time would tell. As of now, all I could do was wallow in pain, because unfortunately I had no one to confide in. Sadly, I was all alone in my home and in my mind, which was the only place I felt safe until Rodney stole that from me too.

DAY 2

The stench from my urine crept up my nose as I woke for the morning. Unaware of the time, I could only guess it was before six a.m. considering that the sun hadn't risen yet. In Georgia, the sun didn't rise until after seven o'clock in the morning. By that time, the sun was already high in the sky and the clouds made way for a clear day in New York.

Although the wetness from the urine had dried, I couldn't pee on myself again, so I got out of bed as soon as the sun rose and lumbered to the bathroom. My bladder was on fire and ready to release and as soon as I touched the toilet seat, a loud stream flowed down. The relief of releasing on a toilet made me feel like a human rather than a pin cushion as Rodney had proven me to be.

Nonetheless, after peeing I sat on the toilet for at least an hour or until both of my feet and upper legs were asleep. I just couldn't move. I was not motivated to do anything, and I damn sure didn't want to look at myself in the mirror. I knew I had to look as much of a mess as I felt, and I didn't need an additional reminder. When I couldn't take the heaviness from my legs being asleep, I slowly raised my body off of the toilet. I limped out of the bathroom, feeling every nerve in my foot until I made it back to my room.

This time instead of getting in bed, I fell on top of a heap of clothing and snuggled under a nearby comforter that I managed to spread over my body. A few hours went by and this time again, I peed on top of the clothes. I watched the urine trickle down my leg and onto the floor, seeping into the cracks of the hardwood tiles. I was all out of tears, and I was at a loss for words and the capacity to feel. Numbness took over my entire body and mental state as I stayed on the floor until the sun set again. My mind was empty, and my heart was completely disconnected from reality; like a piece of garbage, I was discarded into the trash as nothing.

8

DADDY WARBUCKS

SHENELLE "SHELLY" FOX

"**Y**ES BABY, GET ALL IN THAT ASS," SEAN PURRED AS I licked around his booty hole.

Sticking my tongue in and out of his anus was the only time Sean let his guard down and moaned during sex. This was the one position that gave me a sense of power over my dominant Alpha husband. At first, he wasn't with it, but after I made him cum by stimulating the G-spot in his rectum, it was something he became more comfortable with requesting.

It was also my way of breaking him down and keeping his ass in check especially because I was the only ALPHA in this relationship. I didn't care if he was a manly man of Omega Psi Phi, I was the first and the only just like Alpha Kappa Alpha and I wore the pants and ran shit in this marriage. I just let Sean feel like the man, but he was really my bitch. Just like Grandma taught me, "a man is the head, but the woman is the neck, and she can turn the head anyway she wants to" and I lived by that motto.

With Sean's ass tooted in the air, I applied pressure, using my pinky finger inside of his ass and continued licking until he exploded and fell onto his stomach.

"Fuck! Damn babe. That shit be having me moaning like a little ass boy." He panted.

More like my bitch!

"Of course, Wifey knows how to please her man," I said as I crawled on top of his back, turned his neck toward me and kissed him passionately.

"I love you Mrs. Fox, just promise me you won't come out with a tell all book if we ever part ways." He laughed.

"I promise." I joined in on his laugh and latched onto him tightly as I straddled his back.

There was an ingrain woodsy smell that lingered on Sean, especially when he wasn't showered. I inhaled deeply, soaking up his scent. I was the luckiest woman in the world. I had a man who adored me, spoiled me, and allowed me to fulfill my lesbian thirst for women. What more could a girl want? Did I forget to mention that he was the faithful one. In our thirteen years of marriage, it was me who stepped out several times with other women, never him. And never did he seek revenge for my infidelity either, he just allowed me to have my way, and I appreciated that about him.

Sean tossed over, almost crushing me. He stood up and I stayed latched onto him as he carried me towards the bathroom. I may have loved women, but there was no woman or man in the world who could replace my husband. He was perfect.

"Come on baby, get down. We've got to get ready for work," Sean said being his usual pessimistic self.

"I know. I know." I hopped off his back and made my way to my side of our shared bathroom.

"How's Charlie doing? Haven't seen her since we proposed," Sean shouted, his voice somewhat muffled by the running water.

I bit my lip hard, afraid to tell him the truth, so I remained quiet.

"Babe!" Sean shouted again.

Looking at myself in the mirror, I knew I had to be honest with him. I just didn't want him to panic. I put my toothbrush down and cut the water off as I made my way toward him. He was standing with the glass door to the shower open as steam clouded the room.

"What's up babe? I know that look."

The last thing I wanted was Charlie to add any interference between me and Sean's trust, so I just let it out.

"Charlie hasn't been to work in a couple of days."

Sean's eyebrows raised. "What's a couple of days?"

"Today's the fourth day."

"Which is more than a couple," Sean added. "So, when you say she's been out, like she requested the days…?"

My eyes trailed off of his tall stature standing in the shower corridor and returned to the mirror in front of me.

"No call, no show?" Sean bucked.

I nodded my head slowly. "Yeah, babe."

"I told you engaging your colleague wasn't smart. Now she's being insubordinate."

I exhaled, letting the irritation roll off me. Sean just couldn't wait to throw it in my face.

"Nah, babe, I don't think that's it. Charlie's been working for Presbyterian for over five years and has never done this. I think something's wrong."

Sean raised his brows and eyed me suspiciously. "Something like what?"

"I don't know but something just doesn't feel right. Not showing up to work without calling out isn't like Charlie."

"Well did you call her at least?"

"Yeah, several times. It's going straight to voicemail."

"Well, when were you going to tell me?" Sean pressed.

"I'm telling you now."

"Yeah, on the fourth day. I told you about being proactive versus reactive."

Folding my arms and pouting, I rolled my eyes at Sean. He swore he was my fucking father. I usually loved his dominance but occasionally it did come off condescending.

"Babe, you know I always trust your gut and if you're saying something isn't right, then we need to look into it. Pull her address from her file and go check up on her. Hopefully, everything's all right," Sean said through a calming pitch. I loved when Sean was gentle, it reinforced why I married him. Despite his Alpha persona, he was a gentle giant, and he really did have a heart for people. I loved that about him. He was the perfect balance between dominant and submissive and that's what made me continue to fall in love with him again and again. He was the first man that actually knew how to handle me and that's what solidified that he was the one.

I walked over to Sean who was still standing near the entrance of the shower and grabbed him by the neck. Lowering his head to me, I kissed him passionately, circling his lips with my tongue.

"You're right babe. I'll head over there before work."

After parking my Range Rover under Charlie's building, I made my wy into the elevator. It was a cold, brisk day. The air was pretty dry, and the wind was moderate. I was wearing three-inch nude-colored heels and a navy-blue pantsuit. The stench of the parking lot elevator invaded my nostrils, and I instantly covered my mouth. I hated traveling to the Lower East Side. It reeked of sewage, rats, and trash. Charlie made too much money to be living like this. While I understood that living in New York City was expensive regardless to where you were at, no one could have paid me to live here, even when I was making Charlie's salary as a nurse myself.

The elevator finally let me out near the front door of her building. As

I made my way inside the lobby, I was a tad bit confused, as it appeared to be a co-working space. There were at least twenty people, about eighteen of them white, spread out on the chaises plowing away on their laptops. I slid toward the security desk, meeting the young guard who was preoccupied on his smart phone.

I slapped my hand across the desk to get his attention and he perked up, removing his headphones from his ears.

"Good morning, Miss. Who are you here to see?"

"Charlie Thompson, she's in 9C."

"ID please."

I pulled it out of my wallet and handed it over. He glanced it over as he scribbled my name on a handwritten log then passed it back.

"Thank you," I said as I started to walk away toward the next set of elevators.

As I glanced around the building, I noticed that it wasn't that bad. The lights were LED and bright, the marble tiles were well kept, and the intricate free-standing ornaments and wall art added an extra raz-zle-dazzle.

Damn it, Shelly. There I go judging again.

Finally, on the ninth floor, I shuffled off the elevator, and instantly my heart started to race, and my stomach balled up into knots. As I inched closer and closer to her apartment door, my chest tightened and my breathing accelerated, causing me to knock on the door wildly.

"Charlie! It's Shelly! Open up!"

After several knocks, silence resumed. My hands were twitching as I twiddled my thumbs, anxiously waiting on Charlie to stumble to the door. She didn't so I knocked uncontrollably for the next five minutes, almost out of breath until I heard footsteps behind the door.

"Open the door, Charlie. It's Shelly. Sean and I are worried about you."

A minute later, the door creaked open, and a disheveled Charlie stood before me. Her eyes were deranged, under her eyes were black and it looked and smelled like she hadn't showered for days. She eyed me up and down, hollowness written all over her face before she tossed the door open and walked away.

I stepped inside and at first glance, the apartment seemed normal. It didn't smell too bad until I got into Charlie's room and saw the atrocious mess she made of herself. Laying down on a pile of clothes on the floor, Charlie didn't look at me one time. Her closet looked like it had been ransacked. Her mattress looked permanently sunken in and moist. I covered my mouth at a loss for words. Stepping closer toward Charlie who laid out depleted, I kicked my heels off and sat down next to her. As soon as I did, I felt a stream of wetness saturate my pants and seep into the crack of my ass.

I felt icky and disgusting but it was clear that Charlie needed my support and not my judgment at the moment.

Wrapping my arms around her neck, I pulled her closer to me. She rested her head on my shoulder and the heaviness of her entire body fell on me. As she cried softly, I rocked her back and forth. It was obvious something tragic happened, but I wasn't sure how to go about getting the information out of her. She was in no position to talk but I had to know how I could help.

"Did Rodney do this?" I asked softly.

Charlie raised her head from my shoulder and nodded slowly. I looked into her eyes, through the broken fragments of her soul, and my heart shattered.

"He raped me," she revealed. "I've spent the last few days in this exact position trying to figure out how s-so-some-someone I loved so m-mm-much could violate me." Her voice was shaky, and she broke down again.

"It's okay baby. Let it out. I'm here."

"I-I-I loved him. He was the first man I opened up to after my baby father. I told him everything, how Jaden's dad abused me, how I was molested as a child, and he turned around and did exactly that." Her cries intensified, troubling my heart.

"I understand, baby. Trust me, I do. Come on. Let's get you over to our place and cleaned up. I'm here now and you no longer need to suffer.

9

CHARLIE'S ANGELS
CHARLIE

"**A**RE YOU COMFORTABLE? NEED ANYTHING ELSE TO eat? Drink?" Sean asked as he and Shelly crowded around me on my new bed in their guest room.

I nodded my head rapidly, as I was overwhelmed by the care and concern that they had shown me these last few hours. They fed me, bathed me, massaged me, and consoled me while I told my story and continued to cry. Looking into Sean's sympathetic eyes helped me to be more vulnerable. I'd never known him to be such a gentle man, but I was grateful that I had him by my side.

"No. I'm good. You guys have done enough."

"You sure? There's nothing you can't ask for right now that would be too much," Shelly expressed.

"I'm certain. I just want some time alone to think. I bet my son is blowing my phone up like crazy and being that Rodney broke it, he has no way to get in contact with me. Until I muster up the energy to actually go to T-Mobile, I need time to gather the words to tell my son. I'm so scared of what he'd do if I tell him."

Shelly and Sean exchanged looks as they sat on the end of the bed.

"Now might not be the right time to tell him. Isn't he finishing up his last semester in school?" Sean inquired.

"Yeah. He's on track to graduate Summa Cum Laude. He'll be home in three months. I've got to get myself together by then."

Sean brushed his hand over my thigh while Shelly looked at me with big doe eyes.

"There's no specific time frame set for healing. It's a never-ending journey babe. But with our support, I'm certain you'll be in better shape to face your baby," Shelly said, consoling me.

Taking a deep breath, I shook my head rapidly. "If I would have never left here, all of this could have been avoided. But no, I just had to go home. It's all my fault. For being so damn absentminded. For dealing with a man like him." I crumbled and tears streamed down my face. Justin Timberlake's *Cry Me a River* had nothing on me.

Shelly shifted up on the bed and laid next to me. She wrapped her arms around me and rocked me slowly as she kissed my tears. "Don't talk like that! You are not to blame for his coward ass. Nothing you could have done or not done could have prevented this from happening. He wasn't going to leave you alone until he did something bad. Niggas like him never learn."

I settled my cries, as I wiped my face and took in the words Shelly was saying. Hearing her say that reminded me of the first therapist I went to after my virginity was taken from me at twelve years old. At that young age, I couldn't understand what was being said to me. Especially being raised in a strict Protestant family, I grew up thinking every shortcoming was a product of my family's spiritual debt. We were poor because we owed God. Women were raped because they were scandalous. Men were in jail because they were criminals and all we could do was accept it, pray about it, and thank God that things weren't worse. That's how I was raised.

Sean stood up from the bed, folding his arms with a brute countenance. "Charlie, I think you should press charges. This bastard can't get away with what he did."

"Sean, we talked about this already and what pressing rape charges would look like for a black woman, especially in New York where most rapes go unsolved." Shelly intervened.

Pacing back and forth in front of the bed, Sean sucked his teeth. "I've heard and considered what you've said Shellz, but you know I've got high people in high places. We could get this nigga!"

Shelly sat up from the bed, shaking her head. "Well, the final decision has to be made by Charlie."

Turning to me, Shelly pursed her lips. "Charlie, would you like to move forward with pressing charges?"

It was much better listening to them quarrel over me than having to make a tough decision. I know that the relationship we had was unconventional, but I don't know what I would do without these two. They were so well put together. They had a plan for everything. They had each other for support and reasoning. They operated as a team, something I never saw my parents or grandparents do. In the relationships I saw, the man had the final say while the woman wouldn't dare talk back and if she did, the patriarchs in my family had no problem beating the wit out of her, even in front of small children.

"I don't know!" I said exasperated. Having to speak took so much energy. I was depleted, my mind was muddled, and my body was numb. I just didn't know what to do or how to feel.

"Look Charlie, he can't get away with this. Not pressing charges takes all of your power away," Sean asserted.

I lowered my head, trying to conceal the soft cries that fell onto my hands. "He already took it. I have no power left," I bawled.

Shelly wrapped her arms around me again, in a comforting manner. "It's okay, baby. I understand. It's okay."

"I'm going downstairs to the gym. I've got to blow off some steam. This shit is heavy.," Sean sniveled.

"You're right. I think the best thing for you to do would be to give Charlie and I some alone time," Shelly suggested.

"Agreed. After I'm done, I'm going to shower and run to CVS and pick up some dinner. Need anything babe?"

"Yeah, some tissues, chocolate pretzels, Haagen Daagz White Chocolate Raspberry Truffle ice-cream, and some Albanese gummy bears. Oh yeah and some Lays Salt & Vinegar chips. Me and Charlie are going to pig out."

Her statement made me chuckle, which I needed. I needed to laugh again, even if it hurt.

"Got it. Charlie, what do you need?"

"Just some Fig Newtons. The new strawberry kind," I mustered to say.

"How does Thai sound for dinner? I can head downtown to Sea."

"Nah, I'm feeling Greek. Head down to Kellari Taverna. Get my usual and we'll text you Charlie's order in a bit after we look at the menu."

"Cool. Later babes," Sean said before kissing Shelly on the lips and then me on the forehead and exiting the bedroom.

"Don't mind him being pushy for you to press charges. He's just overprotective. He knows when to stop pushing though," Shelly explained.

"Good to know. Shelly, I can't press charges. I can't embarrass my son by carrying on with a trial I just can't bring myself to do it, although I know Rodney deserves to go to jail. I just can't. I can't even bring myself to go back to work right now or set foot in that apartment for anything. I'm just tired."

"I understand baby. As far as work, you don't have to worry about that. I'm going to put in a request for leave of absence for you. The most I can do is three months at a time. Lastly, I'll have someone clean the apartment for you and bring any belongings that you need. If you don't want anything from there, we'll just replace whatever." Shelly couldn't have been more accommodating.

"I don't know how I could repay you. You have opened your home and your heart to me. I feel like I am in a dream."

Pinching the tip of my nose, Shelly chuckled. "Felt that?"

"Yeah."

"You're definitely not in a dream. This is real life Charlie and I love you. I've always favored you since we started working together. I'm just happy that I can help especially in your time of need," Shelly proclaimed as she stroked my leg gently.

"I love you too," I professed before leaning in closer and kissing her on the lips. Everything about Shelly was soft and contained. She was everything I should be, and I admired her femininity. As we kissed softly, she pulled away.

"Charlie, as much as I want you, I only want you whole and at your best self. After experiencing a traumatic sexual assault, the last thing you should be doing is engaging in an increased, unhealthy interest in sex."

The words were flying out of Shelly's mouth quickly, causing my head to hurt. I squinched my nose and leaned closer to her until we were face to face.

"I don't know what to make of what you just said. I just know that when I'm with you, I feel better. When I look at you, I feel safe and when we kiss my heart quickens. I need that right now. I need you, Shenelle," I professed.

With water in her eyes, she fought back tears as she looked at me intently. She exhaled deeply then succumbed to my beckon. Brushing her lips against mine, she nibbled on my bottom lip softly. For what felt like an eternity, we kissed each other and rubbed each other, igniting a sensuality I had never experienced in my life. I was falling in love with a woman.

10

SHADOW WORK

SHELLY

LTHOUGH THE NIGHT WE SPENT TOGETHER AS A trouple felt magical, it was sad to know that a tragedy could bring us closer. I usually enjoyed exploring another woman with my husband but the bond that Charlie and I were building was special. It was one rooted in friendship, sensuality, and vulnerability. While Sean and I had the perfect marriage with transparency, honesty and open communication, the heights that Charlie and I could reach just couldn't compare. Kissing her reminded me of the first relationship I had with a woman, one of my Alpha Kappa Alpha sorority sisters, Shyann. It was slow, it was comforting, and it fulfilled me.

As I rode Sean's dick wildly, all I could think about were Charlie's soft lips. While Sean's hands were firm and hard, I imagined Charlie's gentle touch caressing my body. When Sean flipped me over, fighting for control and dominance, he smacked my ass so hard, it disappointed me. My body was longing for the soft sensuality of a woman. Sean orgasmed and emptied his semen sac into me. Rolling over to the other side of the bed with his back turned to me, he reached for the blanket. Once I heard him snoring and knew that he was fast asleep, I slipped out of bed and made my way to Charlie's room down the hall.

I opened the door quietly, watching her sleep. She was an angel, sleeping so delicately and breathing softly. I slid in the bed next to her and spooned her from behind. She smelled pure with a light natural scent of jasmine. I inhaled deeply, taking in her aroma as I kissed her neck over and over. She never woke up and I was grateful. I didn't want to talk because I didn't know what to say. Charlie was a strong woman who had a child at thirteen and raised him to be a responsible, college-educated man. She had just been sexually violated by her ex and watching her work through her trauma with her vulnerability exposed, made me want to open up to her more.

It was time for me to make a call to Queen Afua and take a trip down to Brooklyn. Charlie was the perfect companion for our sister circle. I just prayed Queen Afua would allow us to come in mid-cycle. It had been years since I completed my first two sister circles, and I haven't been back since. After being introduced to a concept called shadow work by Shyann, I gained a lot of insight about my own childhood traumas and how they were affecting me. Gaining enlightened women as guides and learning how to heal my own womb from traumas changed me. It improved my relationship with myself and helped me to tap into my divine femininity then I met Sean, and the rest was history. I was so excited to embark on this journey with Charlie, guiding her through just as the love of my life had for me.

"Where are we heading Shelly?" Charlie asked as we got off the Brooklyn Bridge. It was a bright and sunny day, with a high of forty degrees which was decent for New York City in February. I always loved the air in Brooklyn. It smelled like culture, not as rich as Harlem but unique in its own way.

"Have you ever heard of the term shadow work?"

Charlie looked over at me from the passenger seat of my Lexus and shook her head. "No. Tell me more."

"We're heading to see a world-renowned healer. Her name is Queen Afua and she's going to help you with your healing journey. Most importantly, she's going to help us to be able to connect on a deeper spiritual level."

Charlie sat mute and her eyes said everything she held back.

"Don't be scared," I joked.

"When you say healer, are you talking about someone who works roots on you?"

I laughed and shook my head. "No nothing like that."

"Are you sure? My ancestors are from New Orleans, and I know all about those roots' ladies. I was told by my Momma to stay away from them. Momma may not have taught me much, but she taught me to stay far away from black magic."

I sighed, exhausted from hearing the ignorance come out of Charlie's mouth.

"Queen Afua does not practice voodoo. Trust me, you're going to be fine. She's a healer that uses natural medicine and the support of a sister circle to help women heal their wombs."

Charlie scrunched up her nose. "So, you're taking me to a healer who's going to fix my womb? So, because I had a child at thirteen and I was raped, my womb is broken!" Charlie screamed, her pitch vibrating through the car.

I reached forward to turn down the radio that blasted advertisements. I grabbed Charlie's hand and squeezed it. She pulled away from me instantly.

"So, that's what you see me as? Your broken womb charity case?"

"No baby, no. It's not that at all. The truth is most black women have womb issues, not just from rape, but from the toxins in foods that we eat and even consensual sex with dirty dick niggas. If it makes you feel any better babe, I have a broken womb too."

Charlie tightened her lips. "You do?"

"Yes, and that's why I'm bringing you here because we have more in common than you know."

"We do?"

"Yes, we do! And I can't wait to reveal it to you. I just wanted to make sure we both had support."

Charlie tilted her head and smiled before placing her hand on my thigh. Thank God things turned around.

"I'm sorry for my outburst Shelly."

"It's all good babe. I know this is all new for you. I also know that getting to know me on such an intimate level is new as well but trust me I'll never hurt you. That's not what I'm here for."

Charlie leaned forward and kissed me on the cheek. "Good to know, because I can't afford any more hurt."

Thirty minutes later, we made it through the bustling traffic down Flatbush Ave and pulled up to Lafayette Street. The feel of Clinton Hill always gave café, bookstore, and art show vibes. Seeing as the area was gentrified with hippies, creatives, and young professionals, this was my favorite part of Brooklyn to frequent. Between attending several shows at Brooklyn Academy of Music including Dance Afrika each May, I was very familiar with this area. Clinton Hill was the only part of Brooklyn I voluntarily went to. Being a Harlem girl kept me uptown and once I started making good money and could afford the lifestyle I really wanted, leaving Manhattan indefinitely never crossed my mind.

After parking the car not too far from Dekalb Ave, Charlie and I strolled down the block hand in hand.

"Do you come to Brooklyn often?"

"Yeah. I love Brooklyn. I wanted to live here, but my place is much closer to the hospital, so I chose the Lower East Side instead," Charlie replied.

"Convenience over luxury. I see. Charlie, I want you to do something for me."

"What's that?" She asked innocently, as I watched her lip curve up highlighting her sexy mouth and lisp she carried. I always loved a woman with a lisp, it just turned me on.

"I want you to never choose convenience over happiness. That shit stops here, because when you're with me, your happiness is my priority."

Charlie blushed, and her cheeks turned rosy red.

"You got me feeling like you're really my man. Damn Shelly, I ain't know you had it like that."

"There's a lot you don't know about me. Best believe, you'll enjoy every minute while finding out," I said as pulled her closer to me and kissed her on the cheek.

"I would have never guessed you were into women from seeing you in the office."

"Good. What about now?"

"It makes perfect sense. You definitely got big purse energy!"

"And do!" I laughed as I pulled Charlie in front of the building.

Squeezing her hand, I turned to her and said, "We're here, you ready?"

"I think so. Should I be scared?" Charlie inquired, raising her eyebrows.

"Never, with me! You're going to leave here a brand-new woman, you'll see."

"Greetings Sister Shelly. Long time no see." Queen Afua was a petite woman in size, but she carried an anointing that reigned supreme. Dressed in white harem pants, and a blue headwrap with spiritual jewelry adorning her wrists, neck, and ankles, she lit up the room.

I leaned forward to capture her embrace. We exchanged pecks on each side of our cheeks.

"Queen Afua, it's so nice to see you. Thank you for allowing me and Charlie to join in mid-session. I know you don't normally do that, but I really appreciate it."

"Ase, sister," Queen Afua said as she crossed her legs and bowed. As soon as she rose up, she reached her hand out in Charlie's direction.

"Greetings and welcome, Sister."

Charlie stepped forward and shook Queen Afua's hand and hugged her. Queen Afua held on to her as she led her through the room. I followed behind, knowing that what existed behind the doors in front of us would change Charlie's life.

The enchanting music that mimicked a soft and consistent lullaby blared through the room as the aroma of sage and mint pursed through my nostrils. I watched Queen Afua guide Charlie through the large circle of women dressed in white linen. I could see Charlie shivering, which was to be expected. I had the same reaction as her my first time. The women who were of all shades and sizes hummed in unison, their voices producing a vibrating pitch that seeped into the depths of my soul.

"Sacred Women." Queen Afua's low pitch was riddled with an equal amount of strength and power that silenced the entire room in an instant without any form of resistance.

The women quieted themselves and faced Queen Afua.

"My apologies for interrupting your divine time. I'm here to introduce a new goddess into the sister circle as well as reintroduce a returning sister. This is Charlie."

"Greetings Sister Charlie," the women said in unison.

Charlie's cheeks puffed out as she covered her mouth, hiding her apparent anxiety. She waved nervously and said "Hi."

"Ladies, welcome Sister Shelly."

"Greetings Sister Shelly."

"Greetings Sacred Women." I said and bowed in respect.

"Make room for the ladies to take a seat, as we invite them in."

Charlie and I both joined the circle. I held onto her as I could feel her nervousness.

"Ladies. We are currently in the third gateway, Sacred Movement. If you are anxious and stressed, sacred movement can bring peace and composure. Sacred movement can empty the body of physical, emotional, and psychological waste. I want you ladies to follow me, as we move through this gateway." Queen Afua announced as she rolled her hips in a circular motion.

"Hear and feel the breath. Let's loosen up our bodies. As you move, I want you to repeat this spiritual prayer. Sacred women in the making, sacred women reawaken. Sacred spirit, hold me near. Protect me from all harm and fear, beneath the stones of life, direct my steps in the right way as I journey through this vision. Sacred spirit surround me in your most absolute perfect light. Anoint me in your sacred purity, peace, and divine insight. Bless me, truly bless me as I share this sacred life. Teach me, sacred spirit to be in tune with the universe. Teach me how to heal with the inner and outer elements of air, fire, water, and earth."

As we released the words, the weight of the world rolled off my shoulders. There was a settled relaxation across all of the women's faces, especially Charlie's. Queen Afua stepped in the middle of the circle with a satisfying grin spread across her mouth.

"Today, we're going to spread some time confronting and releasing our past traumas. As we know when we keep trauma inside, it affects our wombs. The only way for sacred movement and to unblock our wombs, we must release. Many of you were introduced to this practice in Gateway One and you continue it through the use of your sacred womb journal. I want you to reflect on an experience you wrote about in your journal and share it with the circle. This will allow you to re-lease the pain," Queen Afua said, her voice as light and beautiful as a cascading waterfall.

She held her head up and glanced around the circle until her gaze settled on me. "Goddess Shelly, why don't you start? I think your ex-perience having gone through the gateway twice would be of benefit to the ladies."

I swallowed a silent gulp and forced a smile as I stepped forward. Usually, I didn't fear public speaking, as a lot of my work required me to give presentations and speak to large groups of people. But this was different. Staring back at me were souls that harbored hurricanes and damaging tsunamis, the same as me. I choked up slightly trying to weather the storm. I took a deep breath and blocked out the women's faces with a red beam. As long as I stayed focused on the dot, I didn't have to process their expressions.

"Like many of you, I know what it's like to feel pain. It wasn't until I went through my first sister circle ten years ago when I learned that most of the trauma my womb has endured was brought on by me. That was a shocking revelation." I pursed my lips, and inhaled deeply, allowing the words to get stuck in my breath. There was truly no reason to rush as the construct of time didn't exist in Queen Afua's space. There were no clocks on the wall so all we had were time, as it ticked away not worried about any of us, while we didn't worry about her either. My story would take its time to come out and I was okay with that.

"I wasn't raped or sexually violated. I was just promiscuous. I had sex for the first time at fourteen years old. I had a boyfriend all throughout high school and I got pregnant with my first child at fifteen years old. I had my first abortion shortly after. I then got pregnant immediately after my first abortion then had another abortion. Three months later after failing to take my birth control, I became pregnant again and had another abortion. This cycle continued until I had nine abortions by the time I was seventeen. On my eighteen birthday, my boyfriend and I decided that we were going to keep the baby that we were carrying. We had our entire lives planned. We both were accepted to the same college and our parents supported our decision. They even helped us get our first apartment. At twenty-two weeks pregnant, I lost my baby to a harmful miscarriage that almost killed me. A year later I got pregnant again and had a miscarriage at ten weeks. I have been happily married to a wonderful man and have not been able to have a baby, let alone conceive. I beat myself up daily because both me and my husband want children, but it seems like it's nearly impossible for me to get pregnant. The worse thing of all is the guilt that I carry for not only having several abortions but from hiding my past from my husband. I don't know what eats me up more the shame or the guilt."

By the time I finished sharing, tears stained my face as I looked back at watery eyes and sullen expressions on the women's faces. I couldn't bring myself to look at Charlie. This was the most I had shared about myself, and it made me crumble to think that her esteemed opinion of me would change. I felt as naked as I did as a little girl when I had sex for the first time. Although I yearned for sex for the very first time, just as I yearned to show my vulnerability to Charlie, there was still a subconscious throbbing regret that rumbled in the pit of my belly.

Being completely transparent in front of Charlie and a room of strangers gave me the release I needed. It had been years since I faced my demons and it felt good to know that even if I didn't have it in me to bare it all to my husband, I could let my guard down in front of my lover and friend.

11
VIRGIN PUSSY
CHARLIE

THE DOOR SLAMMED AND THE CHURNING OF THE lock alerted me to the company that invaded my privacy. I squealed at his presence. My adolescent body had just started to develop as my hips filled out and my breasts filled in and became heavier over the course of the past year. Eating biscuits with bananas and strawberry jam daily had me thicker than a bowl of oats. Nonetheless, I still wasn't comfortable in my body, and I didn't want anyone to see me naked, especially not my brother Charles' teenage best friend.

"What are you doing in here!" I yelled, demanding answers, as my voice rattled through the baseboards. Our house was one of the oldest homes in LaGrange, so it was impossible to not hear everyone's business. The only thing stopping folks from hearing what went on in our house was the fact that we were in a spaced-out suburb a few acres apart from other homes.

"Shh! Stop all that screaming," Kevin insisted as he stepped closer to me.

I covered myself, squirming towards the bed to reach for my shirt.

Kevin, who was seventeen years old to my twelve, beat me to it and yanked my shirt from off the bed.

"Give it back!"

A sly grin crept up his face as he taunted me, hopping back and forth. "Come and get it!" He egged me on.

Holding my breasts up with my arm, I inched closer toward him and tried to snatch my shirt back.

"CHARLES! Your friend is in here bothering me!" I yelled out.

Kevin, who was tall and muscular threw my shirt on the floor and yoked me up. As he covered my mouth with his hand, I wailed uncontrollably, hitting him with my fists. Using all of his might, he wrapped his hands around my neck and motioned me towards the bed. Out of pure fear, I bit his hand so hard that he jumped back. Swiftly, I ran near the door and picked up my shirt. As I threw it on and attempted to run out of the room, a strong force pulled me away. Strands of my hair felt as if they were being lifted from my scalp as Kevin held a handful of it in a tight grip.

"STOP!" I screamed and kicked as he continued to pull me back.

Just when I thought that fighting wouldn't help, the door creaked open, and I saw my brother Charles. My heartbeat slowed down, and a sense of relief came over me. Charles, who looked like my twin brother rather than my older brother stepped inside the room slowly. Not once did Kevin release me from his grip.

"Charles, please tell him to stop. He's hurting me."

Charles looked at me with flat, dead eyes. "Shut up Charlie. Nobody can hear you anyway. Momma and Daddy won't be back until tomorrow."

I was confused as I shook my head back and forth, fighting back tears. I couldn't believe what I heard.

"Charles, please help me. Please, brother."

Instead, Charles stepped aside, and in came Aaron, Mr., and Mrs. Robinson's boy from down the road. Aaron peeled off three twenty-dollar bills and shoved them in Charles's hand. Greedily Charles grabbed the money and shoved it in his pocket.

Aaron's face lit up as he stepped closer and closer to me. He pinched my nipples and kissed me on the mouth, forcing his slimy tongue down my throat. Disgusted, I bit his tongue as hard as I could, and he jumped back. Almost instantly, he smacked me across the face.

"This fucking bitch is too fussy, and she likes to fight. She bit my hand and just bit Aaron, we didn't pay you one hundred and twenty dollars for nothing," Kevin argued as he continued pulling me by the hair.

I couldn't believe what was going on. My own brother had sold my virginity to his best friends. Tears streamed down my face and the salt peppered my tongue. Anger rose from my fingertips to my knuckles and up my shoulders. I was prepared to fight for my freedom because there was no way I would just allow them to rape me.

"Trust me, everything will be fine. Everybody knows there's no better pussy than when you take it. Especially from one who puts up a

good fight," Charles spat with venom as he kissed his teeth.

Hearing his statement brought out the fire in me and I started swinging and kicking. Aaron blocked his face and moved out of the way. Even Kevin backed up and finally let go of my hair.

"Bro, I'm gon' need my money back. I'm not dealing with this when Sarah from up the block will fuck me with no problem," Aaron objected.

Charles stepped closer to me and punched me so hard in the eye, I saw stars. I tumbled back and Kevin caught me before I fell.

"Nigga, stop bitching. Sarah done fucked the whole block. This is virgin pussy. Pick her up and push her on the bed. I've got some rope to tie her legs down," Charles asserted.

Quickly after I was spread out on the bed with my legs tied to each end of the bedpost and my hands tied to the barred headboard.

I screamed at the top of my lungs repeatedly. Momma and Daddy may have been gone but somebody driving by or walking by was going to hear me. I watched Kevin drop his pants and his gummy limp dick dropped down. This was my second time seeing a penis and it was enormous compared to the first one I saw.

"Please don't. Please don't," I begged, tears clouding my vision and snot coming out of my nose.

"Charles, she's fucking up the vibe with all this crying," Aaron said.

Charles left the room without saying anything and returned a few moments later. His footsteps intensified the dread that loomed in my mind. It wasn't until he tore off a piece of duct tape and plastered it over my mouth, that I blanked.

"That better?" Charles asked.

"Perfect. Now we can enjoy this pussy in peace," Kevin bragged.

"Now hurry the fuck up. Both of you only get fifteen minutes each. This some virgin pussy so it shouldn't take either of you long to nut. If you want to go longer, that's sixty dollars each for another fifteen minutes," Charles said auctioning me off like a slab of meat.

Tears continued to stream down my face, and instead of rattling the bed trying to free myself, I just gave in.

"Charles, you's a greedy motherfucker. Sixty dollars for fifteen minutes and I can't even get no head because you sealed her mouth shut."

"Nigga after she done bit both of you, I don't think trying to get some head would be wise. Now shut the fuck up and get to it. Your time is already dwindling down," Charles announced before leaving the room.

Once the door slammed, Aaron stepped forward and hopped on the bed. "I'm first nigga!" Aaron declared. As he fumbled out of his pants, he hovered on top of me and forced his penis inside of me. The pain hurt like hell and my eyes shot open as I screamed, with no luck as my wails were muffled.

Aaron pumped and pumped, grunting loudly. "He wasn't lying this virgin pussy is good" Aaron continued to pump as I laid under him crushed by the weight of his degradation. A few moments later, he covered my eyes with his hand, smashing me further into the bed as he relieved all of his weight on me. He became rougher with each thrust.

"O-o-o shit!" He yelped as his thrusts rattled the bed. It felt like he was tearing my insides. Being that I couldn't speak, I had to rely on my ears.

Quickly after Aaron fell on top of me, I felt a warm liquid inside of me followed by a burning sensation. Instantaneously, Aaron kissed me on the cheek and smacked my face.

"Nigga move, it's my turn," Kevin shouted.

"Damn, can a nigga catch his breath? I just busted a nut."

"You a stupid nigga busting in her, now what if she gets pregnant?" Kevin asked.

"Shut the fuck up. I ain't never heard of a virgin getting pregnant on her first time. She'll be all right," Aaron retorted.

"You better hope so. My Daddy taught me well. It don't matter how good the pussy is, always pull out," Kevin explained.

"Whatever nigga. As long as I got my nut, I don't give a fuck," Aaron responded as he got up off the bed and began dressing himself.

Kevin shrugged as he jacked his dick a few times then hopped on the bed. For the next fifteen minutes, he tore my insides open as he pumped away. Just as his father taught him, he pulled out just when he was about to finish and splattered the same white liquid all over my face. Between the blood trailing down my leg and the white gunk falling off my face, I never felt more violated in my life.

Tears were flowing heavily as I wrapped up the story for Shelly. She caressed my hand softly as we sat in Imani's, a Caribbean restaurant in Clinton Hill.

"Charlie, you have been through so much. I am so sorry that happened to you," Shelly offered compassion as she continued stroking my hand. Something about her touch and her voice just soothed and relaxed me.

I exhaled a long breath and wiped my eyes with a napkin. "Thank you Shelly. Thank you for everything. I haven't shared this with anyone but Rodney. Not my parents, none of my friends growing up, not my best friend Sade, not even my son. You're really an Angel. Attending the sister circle and hearing your story and seeing how brave you were to share it with a bunch of strangers made me comfortable enough to share my story with you."

Shelly shook her head agreeably. "Let me just say that I am so grateful that I was able to provide a safe space for you to reveal something so private with me. I really think you should continue with the sister's circle as well as some counseling. Queen Afua has a pool of some phenomenal black women therapists that you can take advantage of. And I'll be here every step of the way."

I smiled genuinely. "It's so refreshing to know that I have you by my side especially considering that I want to report the assault from Rodney," I revealed.

Shelly's eyes widened. "Really, babe?"

I pursed my lips and raised my brow as I slowly nodded my head. "Yeah, I'm tired of sparing men that hurt me. It's time to stand up for myself, even if it doesn't result in criminal charges, getting it down on paper and accusing my abuser legally helps me take my power back. And Shelly more than anything, that's what I need," I whimpered.

Shelly got up from her seat and sat down next to me as she pulled me into an embrace. "Whatever you need baby, I am here for you every step of the way."

12
RAINBOW
CHARLIE

"**Y**OU SURE YOU DON'T NEED US TO COME IN WITH you?" Sean asked as we sat in front of the 25th precinct in Harlem.

At first, I contemplated having them by my side for comfort, but some things I just had to face alone.

"No, I'm good. Thanks for the support though."

"Of course, babe. Call us when from the precinct you're done, we'll be nearby," Shelly responded.

I leaned in and Shelly and I exchanged kisses on the cheek before I hopped out of the car. I took a deep breath as I walked into the precinct. Memories of being raped by my brother's friends, getting pregnant with Jaden, and being assaulted by Rodney were floating through my mind all day. The bright stark lights of the precinct shook me out of my destructive thoughts as I approached the desk. Despite the melancholy that permeated in the air, the smell of donuts and coffee, helped to ease the strife.

"How can I help you?" The mid age white officer asked.

"I'm here to report a sexual assault."

The officer lowered her eyes and exhaled. "Okay, have a seat. I'll be with you shortly."

About fifteen minutes later, I was escorted toward the back of the station. Another uniformed officer placed me inside of a room where I knew I was about to be interrogated. He asked me if I wanted something to drink. I said no, then quickly changed my mind.

"I'll have a bottled water and a hot tea with lemon."

I couldn't stand to be parched while recounting this trauma, again and again. I needed some liquid to moisturize the dryness associated with the pain.

"Sure! I'll be right back."

The officer left the room and returned with what I requested.

"Sit tight. The detectives will be in shortly."

I watched the officer leave for good and I stared into the plastic cup of tea. Anxiety had crept up. I hope I was able to get the words out because I was determined to see Rodney be held accountable. Me coming here to report this assault was my restitution for every time I was sexually violated, inappropriately touched, and taken advantage of by men. I had reached my wits end with being abused by men. Rodney was going to pay for this, even if it hurt me to go through with it. Something had to give.

I sat up in my chair after finishing my tea and the door opened. In walked two detectives. One was as old and Jewish as Detective Munch from Law & Order SVU and the other was the complete opposite. She was young, black, and short.

"Hello, Ms. Thompson. My name is Detective Kauffman, and this is my partner Detective Jones. How about we start from the top? What happened on the night of February 11th, 2023?" Detective Kauffman inquired as he squinched his eyes looking at the paper in front of him.

I was grateful that neither one of the detectives attempted to undermine my story or try to blame me for what happened. I told them everything. I told them about the fight Rodney, and I had prior to the rape, which made me kick him out. I told them about my new relationship with Shelly and Sean and how Rodney came up to the hospital to start trouble. I needed them to know everything so they could look into everything. Both detectives nodded their heads and smiled. I had no idea that they wouldn't judge me. I went into the precinct with a false perception of law enforcement, and it actually made me feel bad, especially since they both showed so much care, caution, and concern.

I looked down at the clock on the wall and noticed it had been an hour that I had been there.

"Thank you for coming in Ms. Thompson. Considering that most sexual assaults go underreported, you are brave for attempting to bring charges against your assaulter. With that said, we will contact you once your order of protection is signed off on by the court. In the meantime, we will need you to head to the hospital for a sexual assault forensic exam," said the Detective Munch lookalike.

I scratched my head, slightly confused. "The hospital?"

"Yeah, the hospital. Didn't you say you were a nurse?"

I nodded in agreement.

"When someone is raped and has failed to report it within seventy-two hours, they must adhere to a more robust exam that can reveal other forms of evidence. In order to move forward with prosecution, you must complete this forensic exam."

"Okay," I obliged.

"My partner made a call to Harlem Hospital and they're expecting you. The results from the exam come back in a few days. During that time, we will be investigating Mr. Kane. If he makes any form of contact with you, try your best to record it. If you can't don't worry, just don't forget to call me. I need to be made aware of any contact. It helps your case."

The word case was causing my head to spin. I really didn't know if I had it in me go through with this. I just wanted to report it and tell my story. But I should have known that it wouldn't stop there. Of course, the state would want to prosecute him if they could.

"Okay," I repeated.

"You'll be hearing from us shortly, Ms. Thompson. Let me walk you out," the detective announced as he got up from his seat and headed toward the door. As I followed behind him, I said "Can I use your phone? Rodney broke mine and I have yet to get a new one. I need to text Shelly."

"Sure," the black female officer said as she passed me her cell phone.

I typed in Shelly's number and texted her.

It's Charlie. I'm leaving the precinct now.

Shelly: We're around the corner. We'll be there in a few.

"Thank you," I said as I passed the officer back her phone.

"You're welcome, Charlie. Enjoy the rest of your day and remember that me and Detective Kauffman are only a call away," she said as he handed me her business card. Detective Kauffman handed me his as well and smiled.

"Thank you."

I stuffed both business cards into my purse and exited the building. Within five minutes Sean pulled up in front of the precinct. The sun was shining, and the weather was moderate, reminding me of the fact that spring was nearing. Seeing Sean's fine ass get out of the car and open the back door for me turned me on. I had never looked at him like that, but it was something about his stature, how protective he was and how much he loved his wife and extended that love to me, that made me view him in a new light. Despite how fucked up shit really was, having the Fox's by my side made it all the better. For the first time in the last week, I had finally seen some type of silver lining.

I never thought I'd thank God for all the pain in my life, but the truth was, without it, I wouldn't have met these two angels, who were turning my dark, dreary cloud into a bright rainbow.

"Where to gorgeous?" Sean hollered.

"Harlem Hospital. I have to get examined."

Sean nodded his head as he closed the door behind me. I settled into my seat and was met by Shelly passing me a Starbucks iced Frappe.

"My fave. Mocha Cookie! You remembered!" I squealed.

"Of course, I did. Don't act like our relationship is totally new. We have been working together for five years. I know you like the back of my hand," Shelly jested. "It's Sean that has to get to know you a bit better."

Sean chuckled. "Yeah, that's right, but I think we all need to get to know each other on a more intimate level." Sean pulled out of the parking spot and cruised down the block. I hated driving in New York City because the speed limit was twenty-five miles per hour. That's exactly why I hadn't had a car all of these years. Living in New York, a car was a luxury, not a necessity. In fact, it was also deemed a hassle, between parking, traffic, speeding tickets and the speeding limit. Nonetheless, it felt good to be driven around. That I could get used to.

"Intimate like how? We've already licked each other from the rooter to the tooter and I've shared some pretty vulnerable things with you all," I retorted.

"True, you have. But on a serious note, we need to get tested. All three of us. It's been a while since me, and Shelly have gotten tested, considering that we don't step out of our marriage, and we trust each other. However, by bringing another party in, we should have been gotten tested. Shit, we're medical professionals."

I couldn't lie he had a point, and I wasn't at all offended.

"You're right. Well, how about ya'll get tested while I'm getting the rape kit done?"

"Exactly!" Sean said as he lowered his rearview mirror, and I caught a glimpse of his pearly white teeth. "Great minds think alike," Sean smirked and winked.

I couldn't believe that I was really in a polyamorous relationship with equally romantic feelings for both of my lovers. If someone would have told me that I'd gain a man and a woman after tossing Rodney's ass to the curb, I would have never believed them.

13
CHARLIE'S GROOVE
CHARLIE

I WOKE UP THE NEXT DAY WITH A NEW MOTIVATION. IT had been nearly two weeks since I hadn't had a phone. I knew Jaden was going crazy having not spoken to me. There were probably all kinds of things going on in his head, regarding my safety and whereabouts. He has probably called my phone too many times to count and to no avail. The truth was that I just couldn't find it in me to call him. I didn't know how to tell my son, whom I was responsible for protecting my entire life that I had been violated. I knew that it would have a negative effect on him because he'd feel just as powerless as me, considering that he wasn't there to protect me.

As I entered the bathroom to prepare for my day, I made up my mind that it was time to move on, get a new phone, face my son, and get back to my life. Although there were a few new additions to my life, big additions; Shelly and Sean, I was still determined to get back aspects of my old life. After brushing my teeth, washing my face, and showering, I slipped into a jogger suit and some sneakers and made my way into the kitchen. It was a little after nine a.m. and the condo was quiet, so I knew that neither Shelly nor Sean were there.

While approaching the island in the kitchen, I saw a handwritten letter and a white mailing envelope next to it.

Charlie,

Treat yourself to some shopping. Since we haven't been back to your apartment, I know you're kind of short on daily essentials and everyday clothes. While you're at it, also pamper yourself. Nails, toes, brows, facial, lashes, and hair. I have a pretty busy week since I was out a few days last week, so I can't make it with you this time. Nonetheless, Sean and I still want you looking and feeling your best.

Enjoy your day beautiful.

-Shellz

I smiled as I picked up the envelope and counted out five thousand dollars. Although, I had an account full of money, it was nice to not have to spend my own, especially considering that I still had bills to pay at my house. Now that I was living with Sean and Shelly, I decided that I would give Jaden my apartment when he moved back home. I would cover the rent for a year and even redecorate the apartment for him. His job was set to start immediately a month after he graduated, and he'd be starting at seventy-thousand dollars a year. He'd be able to take care of himself and if he ever needed me, I'd be right here to help him.

I just hope that he'd be able to handle living as a true adult on his own, because truthfully him living on his own right away was never a part of the plan. Either way, I was sure he'd like to have his own apartment and I was just happy I was able to set my baby up. I came a long way from a nappy headed girl from LaGrange, Georgia who started out as a CNA making nine dollars an hour. I was damn proud of myself and my son. Today was going to be a great day. As soon as I got my new phone, I was going to call my baby immediately.

I strolled down 34th Street carrying several bags from Old Navy, Forever 21, and Zara. Each and every one of the stores had its spring collections laid out. Springy greens, and pastel pinks, and yellows populated the merchandising areas of each store. I racked up on essentials like tank tops, joggers, and other house clothes from Old Navy while I scored some chic looks from Zara and some everyday pieces from Forever 21. If I had the energy in me, I would have gone into Herald's Square Macys, but I needed a partner for that level of shopping.

Seeing as it wasn't quite noon yet, the usual hustle and bustle on 34th Street was not nearly as overwhelming. I peeked inside T-Mobile and noticed there were only three customers there with eight open kiosks. *Perfect.*

"Welcome to T-Mobile. How can we help you?" A young, gay Spanish guy sporting a turquoise blue mohawk asked.

"I need the newest iPhone!"

"Do you have an account with us already?"

"Yes. I do."

"Let me have your number and ID please!"

I gave him my number and ID and patiently waited as he typed away on the computer.

"Got you all pulled up, Ms. Thompson. Are you interested in an installment plan for your phone? We have two options."

"No installment. I want to pay for the phone in full and with cash. Include a Screen protector and an Outterbox case."

"My favorite kind of customer!" He smiled. "Would you also like to purchase headphones and a charger? The newest iPhone doesn't come with either."

My half-smile turned into a frown, which I quickly caught. Although that pissed me off, it was time that I recognized that I had money and stopped allowing petty bullshit surrounding finances to get to me. Not only did I come a long way on my own from penny-pinching, Piggly Wiggly and, Kool-Aid, I now had two people who cared for me and even assumed full financial responsibility for me. All I had to do was take care of my son and I was more than capable of that.

With my lips pursed, I inhaled through my nose. "All the bells and whistles. I need everything!"

After paying the associate, he set my phone up and I was out of there within forty minutes. Seeing as I had the same number, I wasn't out of the store for five minutes before it rang, and I noticed the unsaved number was Jaden's. I held my breath before answering. I knew this wasn't going to be the most pleasant conversation, but I had more than enough time to prepare for it.

"Hello," I answered with a cheeky smile, hoping to soften the blow.

"Hello? That's all you have to say? Where the fuck have you been Ma? I've been worried." Jaden wasn't lying, the irritation in his voice told me everything.

"Baby, I know you're upset but my life has literally been a wreck these last two weeks. Rodney and I got into a huge fight. He's been stalking me, so I left the apartment and have been staying at Sade's." I fibbed.

Jaden was breathing heavily and kissing his teeth. From the low growl in his voice, I could only imagine his seething anger festering. So, before he could respond, I beat him to it.

"But don't worry, everything is being handled. Police is involved and they've issued me an order of protection until they arrest him. He has no idea where I'm at and we haven't been in contact. The reason my phone hasn't been on is because he broke it. I just got a new phone a few minutes ago. I'll be changing my number shortly, so he has no contact with me."

"Ma, I swear to God this shit with you and him has been getting out of hand. What the fuck is a new number going to change? That ain't gon' stop him."

"Baby, trust me I'm handling it."

A FaceTime call from Jaden came through.

"Answer me ma, I need to see your face," he demanded.

I answered it quickly and I immediately regretted it. Frow lines and dark circles covered my baby's face. He was really worried about me. It hurt to see him like that, especially when I could have just picked up the phone and called him. I felt horrible, like an unfit terrible mother. Even though my baby boy was grown, it didn't hurt any less to know that my actions caused him severe distress.

I smiled and softened my eyes. "It's so nice to see you baby. I promise I won't ever have you worrying like that again."

Jaden's nostrils were flaring, and I saw hair inside of his nose as he had the camera so close to his face.

"Ma, I've been worrying about you since you got with that clown. Learning that he abuses you doesn't make it any better."

"Look Jaden, I told you I'm handling it."

"YOU'VE BEEN SAYING THAT FOR THREE YEARS! And it's just been getting worse. I think it's time for me to handle it!" Jaden bunched his lips up and tightened his jaw.

"NO! NO, baby. I am your mother. It's not your job to fight my battles. You have enough to fight as a young black man in this white's man world. I've worked hard to ensure you stayed on the right path since coming home from juvie. Look at you. You're about to graduate college summa cum laude with several job offers. I have laid down my life for you to have a shot at all of these opportunities. You will not fuck that up for me and the horrible choices I've made in men. That is not your burden to carry!" I asserted, nearly screaming in the phone as I waited in front of the 2 and 3 trains on the corner of Seventh Ave and 34th Street. I didn't care who heard me. Besides New Yorkers always minded their business and for that I was grateful at this moment.

Now Jaden was scowling. "Ma, I don't give a fuck about none of that. You are all that I care about. I can't allow some sucker ass nigga to keep putting his hands on you. Part of me believes he only been trying that shit since I've been away. And that shit ends today. I don't care what you say. I'm stepping to that nigga, so just stay at your friend's house and lay low. May will be here in no time, and I promise you when I see that nigga, his ass gon' make it on the news and on a t-shirt. Pussy ass nigga!" Jaden seethed.

I hadn't heard him talk like that in a long time and nothing about it made me feel good. I knew there was nothing I could do to stop him. Once Jaden made his mind up about something, there was nothing that could be done to change it. The only thing I could do was hope that Detective Kauffman would get to Rodney before my treacherous, over-protective son had.

Aside from the disturbing call that I had with Jaden; my day was going pretty well. I called Sade and lied to her also, just to put her mind at ease. I know she was worried sick about me. After dropping off my shopping bags, I decided to take a trip to the grocery store. I was feigning for some soul food. The least I could do for the Fox's was show them some southern hospitality. Considering how they welcomed me into their home, I could make them a meal.

I was an amazing cook. That was one of the things that hooked Rodney so fast. As soon as he tasted my six-cheese truffle mac and cheese and my sweet, candied yams, he fell in love. But the truth was that I hadn't cooked for him in over a year. Everyone knew that soul food came from the heart. If your heart wasn't in it, the food wouldn't be good. And I checked out of the relationship with Rodney a while ago. Being the breadwinner, working long hours and coming home to a dirty house didn't inspire me to cook for a man who wasn't my husband.

But thinking about how my life had changed since Shelly welcomed me into her marriage gave me the incentive to want to cook. Once I got back home, I turned on some soft R&B and got to boiling my turkey necks and cutting up my greens. It was three o'clock and neither Shelly nor Sean were expected to be home before seven p.m., so I had more than enough time to prepare my dinner.

Hours later, the aroma of homemade country cooking filled the air, and the dining table was set with mac and cheese, candied yams, turkey wings, collard greens and homemade strawberry biscuits. I even made a peach lemonade and sweet tea from scratch. I spruced myself up, curled my hair and put on a bit of makeup I picked up from Sephora. It was now a quarter until eight p.m. and the rattling sound of keys approached the front door.

"We're home!" Sean and Shelly yelled in unison as their footsteps persisted forward.

"Damn, girl it smells good as fuck in here!" Sean shouted.

"It sure does! Our baby knows how to throw down!" Shelly squealed, as they turned the corner.

Although they had been out of the house for over twelve hours, they still looked fresh. The Fox's were one attractive ass couple. They complimented each other well and it was important to me that I stepped my game up. I had not only one person, but two people's attention to keep.

"Wow. A feast! This looks almost as good as you!" Sean complimented me as he stepped forward and pecked me on the lips.

It warmed my heart to be greeted with such care.

"You curled your hair and you're wearing lipstick and that new Fenty highlighter." Shelly noticed as she winked her eye. "I love it, baby," she said as she stepped forward and kissed me with a little more passion as she squeezed my ass. My pussy jumped for the first time since I was assaulted. I couldn't even think about sex until today but being with these two brought out a heightened sense of sexuality I didn't know I needed.

Sean shimmied inside of the dining room and pulled out a chair.

"Aht aht. Wash your hands first. Both of you!" I teased.

"Alright Mommy Dearest!" Sean joked and we all laughed.

It felt good to be a part of a loving family.

14
MY MAN
SHELLY

"**D**AMN! *NO MORE RIGHT NOW, I NEED A BREAK*," Sean begged us as me and Charlie laid on each side of him in the bed. Sean had just orgasmed twice, back-to-back. One nut he shot inside of me, and the other Charlie swallowed. But Charlie and I were still ready to go. In fact, Charlie was practically begging for more.

"All right Mr. Tap Out," I joked as I crawled over him and saddled on top of Charlie. "Move over!" I demanded playfully while nudging Sean in the side.

He tossed and turned as he scooted over to the naked side of the bed. Sitting comfortably on top of Charlie, I looked into her lust-filled eyes and immediately my nipples hardened. She licked her lips and smooched at me, which drove me crazy. I lowered myself on her, our lips melting into each other, as we kissed ravishingly. Her delicate fingers rode up my lower back as she caressed me gently. The warmth erupting from our body heat while we rolled around on the bed intensified the passion between us.

Seconds later, Charlie was now on top of me taking control. She wasn't very good at it, but I enjoyed every moment as she explored my body. As she inched down on the bed, licking me in between soft pecks, my body began to shiver. I began to quiver, as vibrations traveled all the way from the soles of my feet to my fingertips. Charlie, who had no prior experience with a woman had touched me in a way Sean was never able to. As she kissed the insides of my thighs, my upper body shook, causing Sean to turn and face me. My eyes rolled into the back of my head as soon as she parted my pussy lips. The moistness from her tongue spread across my pussy effortlessly like a pro ice-skating queen. She lapped up my clit and flickered it with the tip of her tongue while blowing on it gently.

"Yes. Yes. Yes," I panted faintly.

Charlie was eating me like I was the last supper. Savoring me, pleasuring me like a hearty bowl of garnish. While I was in the moment, I couldn't help my mind traveling back to my first love, Shyann. Although masculine, she was so beautiful, I called her my little flower. Shyann was my first and the only woman I loved. She was the only woman that knew just how to touch me, causing my body to go into a shock. The way Charlie was making me feel reminded me so much of Shyann. For the first two years of our relationship, I swore we were going to get married. I even proposed to her, but this was fifteen years ago before gay marriage was legal. We both laughed at it because we knew it was never possible and then I met Sean, who looked at me the same way he was looking at me now, in awe.

I opened my eyes, and there he was staring at me as my body combusted and contorted in ways he was just incapable of unlocking within me. I licked my lips as Charlie licked my pussy. Sean's mouth was slightly ajar as he watched on. We didn't say one word to each other but a few seconds later he inched over and grabbed me in with his lips. Our breaths connected and I knew he could feel me orgasming. I bit on his bottom lip, not letting it go, following Charlie's rhythm down below.

I gasped loudly as I felt my clit throb, releasing the sweet, savory cream I had been holding in for some time. Sean, knowing that I had orgasmed and knowing what I needed next, got on top of me and shoved his dick inside my mouth. As it grew and grew, he fucked my mouth viciously.

"Keep going! Keep going!" I heard him instructing Charlie and so she continued licking and licking. White clouds invaded my mind and the sound of loud trumpets pegged on my eardrums. I kicked and kicked, trying to push Charlie off of me but she wouldn't budge.

"Don't stop and don't let her get away," Sean said.

I couldn't see a thing. All I tasted was the precum from Sean's dick trickling down my throat. I loved when he tea bagged me. It intensified my orgasm especially when I had my pussy in another woman's mouth. My husband knew me so well. I felt myself creaming again as Sean pounced up and down, forcing his thick dick in my mouth. He inched back, unblocking my vision and allowing me to see. As I looked up, I saw the pleasure on his face which made me lock my jaw tightly around his dick. He whimpered and squirmed until I swallowed every last drop of his semen again. He fell on top of me and then rolled off of me before spooning me. As he rested his chin on my neck, Charlie climbed to the top of the bed and settled next to me as I spooned her. We all fell asleep like the banana split we were.

The next few days were full of good sex, good food, and orgasms. I never thought that I would find myself getting burned out from sex, but Charlie had me beat. It was like her sex drive went through the roof. Being that she was on a leave of absence from work, she wanted to fuck three times a day. Sean and I woke up to sex and went to sleep after sex. Not to mention, Charlie was blowing up our phones with all kinds of racy images. She would even facetime us both in a sexy cosplay outfit, while she played with her pussy. She was a real freak and really enjoyed both of us. Between her sexy voice and body, she kept us both enticed.

In fact, her intense sex drive increased ours and enhanced the relationship between me and Sean, not only sexually but professionally. We got along better; our meetings were swifter, and Sean had even secured a multi-million-dollar donor for the hospital. David Koch had been on Sean's radar for some time, but his final meeting with him a few days ago solidified the deal. Sean was so happy when he came home and gave us the news, informing us that his new donor would be honored at this year's Gala and Silent Auction. Watching Sean's face beam with a bright smile warmed my heart. Success looked great on my man, and I had Charlie to thank for that as well. Since she'd been around, Sean's been chipper, and spending more time in the gym. He knew he had to stay in shape to handle us both and watching him do so effortlessly as well as excel at work turned me on. Regardless of how much I craved women, I would never trade in my husband. He was the exemplar of masculinity and strength and despite how much money and power I had, I still needed a man, and I was thankful I had one.

As I cleaned myself up after a Facetime sex session with Charlie, I got up from my desk and switched out my pumps for some flats. The weather was breaking, and I had enough time to run to Hale & Hearty and get a soup and salad before my next meeting. I slipped out of my office and made my way to the elevator. Once I was on the ground floor, I stepped out of the double doors and was met by a brisk breeze. I closed my suit jacket to block out the cold air. Just as I cut the corner, I felt a tight grip on my arm. I turned around instantly and saw Charlie's ex, Rodney. He rushed me into the alleyway where the ambulances pulled in for the emergency room. The tightness of his jaw, the cold in his eyes, and the hollowness written all over his face told me that he hadn't slept in days. His appearance alone scared me.

"Where the fuck is Charlie? She's not at home and I've been watching this hospital day and night for the last few weeks. I haven't seen her come or leave."

I snatched my arm away from his quickly and he forced his arm

across my chest, locking me deeper into the corner. There were no ambulances nor hospital security in sight which was perfect for whatever
crazy ass plan he concocted.

"Look motherfucker, if you ever and I mean ever put your hands on
me again, it won't go well for you. I'm giving you one last chance to
get the fuck off me."

In a matter of a millisecond, Rodney pulled out a boxcutter and held
it to my throat as he leaned in closer. He was so close to me, that I
smelled his hot, foul breath all over my face.

"Bitch, you think I'm scared of you because you got a fancy little
position at this hospital. Man fuck you and your bitch ass husband.
Now I'm going to ask you again, where the fuck is Charlie?"

I gritted my teeth and pursed my lips. Fear had permeated my entire
body. My heart was beating fast, and my palms were sweating. I felt a
tear coming on, but I held it back. I refused to give that motherfucker
the satisfaction of me panicking more than I already had.

"Charlie took a leave of absence from work over a month ago. I
haven't heard from her since. That's why you haven't seen her around."

Rodney's nostrils flared as he rolled his neck and removed the blade
from my jugular. "You better not be lying bitch, because if you are, next
time you won't be so lucky. I just may have to scar that pretty little face
of yours," he spat with venom as he slowly backed up from me and
made a dash out of the alleyway.

Trembling, I pulled out my phone immediately and sent out a group text to Sean and Charlie.

911. Rodney just showed up to the hospital looking for you. He threatened me with a knife.

Sean: WTF? Babe, are you okay?"

I'm all right, just a little shaken up. He didn't hurt me.

Charlie: OMG. I'm so sorry. This is all my fault.

Don't apologize for that jackass. He's the predator. He's the only one to blame.

Sean: Look, Charlie your ex is way out of line and things have gone too far. I'm afraid that I'm gon' have to handle this. We tried your way, but still haven't heard anything from the police about your order of protection. Now he's fucking with my wife. I won't stand for that. Shenelle, take your ass home now. I'll be there shortly.

15

PEBBLE BEACH

DESEAN "SEAN" FOX

"*CHARLIE, I DON'T THINK THIS ARRANGEMENT WITH* you is going to work. I like you and all but having you around is just too risky for me and my wife!" I fumed as I stood with my arms folded. Looking back at me were Charlie's bugged eyes, nearly popping out of her eye socket. Her mouth was slightly ajar as she stared at me in awe.

"Babe, stop. We can't punish Charlie for this crazy ass man and his deranged actions. I'm going to speak with the head of security to assign two personal guards to follow me as well as provide additional security surrounding the perimeter of the hospital. Don't worry! I've got it all under control. This won't happen again!" Shelly assured me with her matter-of-fact tone that she used during meetings and big presentations.

"Shelly, I don't give a fuck about what you're saying. I'm your husband and it's my job to protect you. That nigga went way too far. There's no way I'm allowing you to handle it."

Charlie got up from the sofa and stood in the middle of the living room with her hands covering the sides of her face. "Sean, I'm sorry. I know that my life is messy and complicated and the last thing I want to do is get you two in the middle of my drama," she apologized.

"It's a little too late for all of that. Your ex has proven to be a dangerous, loser type of nigga. He done went upside your head before, he sexually assaulted you, and now he's threatening my wife! I can't let that slide."

"I don't expect you too, just please give me another chance," Charlie pleaded.

I shook my head back and forth deliberately. "I'm sorry but I can't. I can't afford for something worse to pop off. Outside of the fact that he's dangerous, being associated with him isn't good for our image. One of the largest donors in the city just signed off on a one hundred-million-dollar contract for Presbyterian," I iterated. "I just think it would be best if you leave."

Charlie lowered her head and inhaled deeply, and the sound of her breath rattled me. Before she could say anything, Shelly jumped to her defense. Strutting forward as she crossed each leg over the other, one of her sexy signature moves, she stood in front of me demanding my eye contact.

"Babe, you know how much it turns me on when you become super protective of me. But I need you to open your heart and extend that same protection to Charlie. She needs us. She doesn't have a Superman who wears a huge cape like you," Shelly pleaded as she simpered. Her soft glossy eyes lowered to mine as she wrapped her hands around the back of my neck.

I exhaled as I kissed my teeth. Shelly always knew the right words to say to tug my heart and get what she wanted. It usually worked but this time, I had no problem resisting.

Holding the sides of her face in my hand, we touched foreheads while staring intently in each other's eyes. "Baby, I don't know what I would do if something happened to you, and I don't want to find out. Charlie has to go and that's my final answer."

I released her from my embrace, and she stammered right in front of me as tears filled her eyes.

"But, babe, we can't do that. If something happens to Charlie, I won't be able to forgive myself... or you."

My blood was boiling as I processed the lengths Shelly would go to mindfuck me so she could get what she wanted. Trying to guilt-trip me for a favorable outcome was an old trick of hers that we've addressed several times in therapy. How the fuck could she undermine me in front of Charlie?

But like always, I swallowed my pride and chalked it up to manhood. Because it was apparent how much Shelly cared for Charlie. And I couldn't afford to create any waves that would affect our relationship or pull us apart. I loved Shelly more than life itself and I needed her. I may have been the first and only black CEO of New York Presbyterian Hospital, but without my wife, I was nothing and I couldn't do it without her. Not to mention, I was still deeply in love with Shelly, more than she was with me for sure, and she knew this.

So, whatever I had to do to keep her happy, I was willing to, of course within reason.

"All right she stays, but I'm also getting security to watch the penthouse and I've got a trick or two for that nigga Rodney," I said staring Shelly directly in the face. Shelly's eyes lit up as she held on to every word I said. "Just call me Simon the Superman and whatever Simon says, goes. And I won't go easy on his ass either, Charlie. So, whatever happens to your ex, be prepared to live with it!" I seethed, looking intently at Charlie with a raised eyebrow and a nasty smug painted across my lips.

Dressed in a wool Nike Tech suit, some ACG boots, and a ski-mask, I pressed the gas hard as I rode up the Westside Highway to my old stomping grounds- Lincoln Projects. I knew just the right nigga to check in with that would handle this shit with Rodney. Considering that I was heading to Harlem, it was important that I fit in with the locals. The last thing I needed was to get spotted in a suit and cufflinks and then posted all across social media and the news. Fox 5 would have a field day. I could see the headline now: NY Presbyterian Hospital CEO Sean Fox posted up with Hoodlums" plastered on every station that Fox 5 owned. To avoid that, I had to look the part as well as meet Cease in a secret location.

I pulled my Nissan Altima into the parking lot near Madison and 136th street. This was the oldest car I had and the first one I bought in all cash as a senior studying at Columbia University. My baby was still in tip-top shape at one hundred and fifty-nine miles. Blending in meant that I also couldn't drive an expensive ass vehicle in the hood. Not only did I want to avoid the press, but I also wanted to make it out alive. Showing up too flashy in the hood was the surest way to get killed. I may have lived off Central Park West, but I still knew the code of ethics when it came to the street.

After parking my car, I grabbed my black North Face bookbag and made my way to the location Cease told me to meet him at. Once on the fourteenth floor of 2101 Madison Avenue, my stomach started to jitter, and my hand was twitching like usual whenever I was nervous. As I headed up the final flight of stairs towards the roof, I felt an increasing breeze and heard the wind rattle, which informed me that the door was open and Cease and his gang were expecting me. I stepped through the door onto Pebble Beach, the nickname all project kids called the roof across every borough. We called it Pebble Beach because back in the day it used to be full of small, pebbled rocks and it sounded exotic when coaxing girls up there. Most young girls lost their virginity on Pebbles Beach, while most boys were initiated into a gang on the same turf. Not to mention, it was a getaway for most d-boys when dodging the police, especially if two buildings were connected by the roofs. A criminal could easily cross the roof and escape into the next building.

Throughout the years, the roof became hot as police became hip to all of its secret hideaways. Nonetheless, if you ran things like Cease and his crew, the police never bothered you because they were usually on payroll.

"Long time no see, Corporate," Cease greeted me as he stood with his red bloody bandana covering most of his face. Crowded around him were five young boys who were all taller than him. They stepped back, giving Cease some space to approach me. No more than four foot eleven inches tall, Cease made up for the height he lacked in his demeanor and power. Whatever he said went, and it's been that way since I was a teenager. He may have been pushing fifty years old, but he kept an army of young cats around as muscle. Cease was Dominican and the only nigga in the hood that was allowed to breathe after leaving the Trinitarios gang and becoming blood. Everyone respected him, the Trinitarios, the Bloods, the Crips, and the Latin Kings. His name rang bells in the hood, and he was usually the peace officer between all the gangs. If any gang had an issue with the other, Cease would work out a favorable resolution for both sides.

I dapped him up to show my respect and said, "Thanks for seeing me on such short notice."

"It's all good, talk to me."

I took off my bookbag and his army perked up, eyeing me suspiciously. It was dark outside but where we stood was illuminated by several lights which made it easy to see the menacing smugs on his army's faces. I slowly placed the bookbag on the ground and one of his young cats grabbed it immediately and opened it.

"From my estimate, it's at least fifty thousand in here."

"It's double actually. One hundred thousand dollars. I need you to step to this nigga named Rodney Kane. He's from Jefferson Projects. No kids, moms dead, nobody will miss the nigga."

Cease scratched his chin and paced back and forth in front of me. "Jeff is our turf. The entire east side is. I got to look more into this nigga to make sure he's neutral and not affiliated. No amount of money is worth a casualty right now. Feel me, Corporate?"

"Trust me the nigga is neutral. He ain't no killer. He beats women and he's a rapist. Real loser type nigga." I stressed.

"Sounds personal. Who did he rape?"

"My girlfriend."

Cease's eyebrow raised. "Ain't you married to that fine ass bougee chick?"

I chuckled and Cease did too. "No disrespect, Corporate, just wondering."

"Yeah, me and wifey are into poly relationships. We've got a girlfriend. This nigga was her ex. He used to beat her ass and he raped her."

Cease nodded his head repeatedly. "So, this is very personal. Ahh, okay."

"I really didn't want to get you involved, since my girl is in the middle of pressing charges on him, but the nigga stepped to my wife, and pulled a blade out on her. His ass got to be dealt with."

Cease's eyes widened, popping out over his tied bandana that only revealed his orbs. "Say less. We'll handle it!" Cease assured as he rubbed his hands together.

I nodded my head. "Good, just don't kill the nigga. I can't have that on my conscience."

Cease laughed hysterically as he turned to face his army. "Ya'll heard him, right? Put that pain in but leave the nigga breathing."

"Say less OG. We got it!" The young cat that held the bookbag affirmed while nodding his head slowly.

16

A WORK OF ART

SEAN

Three Weeks Later...

SHELLY STOOD IN FRONT OF ME LOOKING ELEGANT as always, in a hip hugging gown with a high slit on the side that revealed her sexy, toned thighs. "Babe, can you help me with this necklace?"

"Sure!" I exclaimed as she handed me one of my favorite diamond pendants that I bought her a few Valentines Days ago. She turned around revealing her slender back and I placed the pendant around her neck, while inhaling her regal parfum. It didn't matter what we went through, this woman still had a hold on me.

"Thanks babe," she said as she hurried in front of the floor length mirror to gage her finished look.

As I watched her prance and pose in front of the mirror, I felt my phone vibrate inside of my suit jacket. I pulled it out and a text from a nondescript number appeared. I opened the message and was met with a picture of Rodney, whose mouth was busted open with blood draining out, left eye protruding out of his eye socket and a slab of fatty tissue ripped out of his cheek.

Damn. They went crazy on him.

Anonymous: Mission accomplished.

Good Looks.

Shaking my head, I shoved my phone back in my pocket after texting back. Shelly was on me like white on rice.

"Who was that babe?" She asked.

"Just my assistant prepping me on how things are looking at the MoMa. She's really outdone herself. She deserves a bonus for her persistence at getting through to David Koch's assistant. If it weren't for Chacha, tonight wouldn't even be happening," I exaggerated.

Shelly sashayed over to me and fixed my collar. As she motioned down my neck and straightened my bowtie, she pressed her finger to my lips. "If it weren't for you and your big ideas, your well executed plan and charm, tonight wouldn't be happening. Tonight, is about you, not your assistant, or anybody else. Remember that baby," she gushed as she kissed me passionately.

It was those words of affirmation and her undying support and belief in me that kept me going. Truthfully, if it weren't for Shelly, I would have never even met David Koch two years ago. It was due to Shelly's sorority sister, that we were invited to his annual brunch at the Trump Golf Links at Ferry Point.

"You always know the right words to say baby. What would I do without you?”

“I have no idea,” she chuckled, and I joined in.

Seconds later in walked Charlie, wearing a champagne A-line dress that gave her a regal elegance that I had never witnessed. Her look had Shelly written all over it. I was almost certain that Shelly had picked it out for her.

“You look beautiful,” Shelly complimented her as we both watched her strut back and forth, tooting and toting her ass in that dress. Charlie was cute, but she didn’t have that oomph that my wife had. Truthfully, I would have never looked Charlie’s way. There was just no extra spark about her to get my attention. She was only in our lives because of Shelly’s lesbianism. The truth was that I was naturally monogamous. I only agreed to polyamory to fulfill Shelly’s need for sensuality with another woman. It didn’t bother me because I preferred her interest in women to perhaps her wanting to step out with men. Nothing and I mean nothing would allow me to accept that.

“Thank you. You look amazing as usual,” Charlie said to Shelly laying it on thick. Although I had forgiven her for getting us caught up with her loser ass ex, I still wasn’t feeling her all too well. As I studied her physique something about her seemed different and it was more than the classy dress, expensive jewelry and sophisticated updo.

“You’re far too kind,” Shelly responded as she leaned forward and pecked Charlie on the lips. The kiss was quick, yet personable, which didn’t make me jealous. Shelly just had that personable flair that made anyone she spoke to comfortable.

"You're looking good too, Mr. CEO," Charlie said as she walked over and kissed me on the cheek. I was so grateful that she didn't try to kiss me on the lips. I still wasn't feeling her ass, no matter how good and extra thick she was looking.

"Our driver will be here in ten minutes, so spray your last bit of parfum and touch up your lipstick ladies, we've got shoulders to rub tonight," I said confidently as I stood in front of the floor length mirror admiring how good I looked. Charlie stepped in front of me rubbing her fat ass on my crotch, and I couldn't help but notice how much heavier it felt and how wide her hips had spread. Interrupting me from fantasizing about tearing Charlie up, was Shelly kissing the side of my neck. Looking back at me in the mirror were three sexy motherfuckers. I made them look good and they made me look even better, especially my wife.

Paparazzi swarmed the black Suburban that we stepped out of in front of The Museum of Modern Art. Flashes of light hit me as I moved swiftly through the photographers and press. Charlie and her date, one of my associates followed behind us. A few days ago, we informed Charlie that she'd be accompanying the Gala with one of my colleagues just for technicality. As the only black couple to lead New York's most prestigious hospital, it was imperative that we kept our personal business under wraps. As far as the public was concerned, Charlie was simply our Director of Nursing, who happened to be on a leave of absence. Nonetheless, nothing in the world would cause her to miss this event, just in case we had to explain her presence, not that we had to.

We waltzed into the museum's lobby which was decorated beautifully, with art pieces spread about. Men and women, mainly white with a sprinkle of pepper were dressed in cocktail dresses and black suits as they paraded from piece to piece. Some scribbled on a notepad that lay in front of the art pieces while others viewed conspicuously and moved on to browse other pieces. Mellow jazz at a moderate volume filled the room while the rambunctious whispers of heels click-clacking and Oxfords shining the floor persisted a mile a minute.

"The man of the hour has arrived," said Daniel, my Latino project manager. Daniel was dressed in a thin black turtleneck sweater, black slacks, and slip-ons, his usual attire even in the office.

"My man," I said as I greeted Daniel and shook his hand.

"Good evening Mrs. Fox, you look darling as always," Daniel said complimenting Shelly and leaning in to peck her on the cheek. They exchanged kisses and Shelly smiled.

"Aww thank you, Daniel. It's so nice to see you. It's been a while," Shelly grinned.

Looking over my shoulder, I saw Charlie and her date Travis holding cocktails and mingling. Seeing as Charlie was the Director of Nursing and our girlfriend, she was the only member of the nursing staff here. The rest of the staff present at tonight's gala were from the

Executive department along with the very important people on our Board of Trustees.

"Yes it has. Your husband keeps me very busy, I'm usually always ordering food for a working lunch, which explains why you haven't seen me around the hospital much," Daniel explained.

"Makes sense. I know it all too well. I don't get out much for lunch either," Shelly went on. "Anyway, I'll leave you two be. I know you have a lot to discuss."

Daniel smiled and so did Shelly before she turned to me and said "I'm going to check out some of the pieces and mingle with the guests. Text if you need me, babe," she cooed as she leaned forward, and we exchanged a friendly kiss.

I turned to Daniel, "Give me a run down," I requested.

"Everything is going as planned. Most of the items have at least ten bids on them. Chacha is manning over check-in and making sure everyone has their seat designation. We have an hour until the Gala starts. Koch and his team aren't here yet, but they are enroute. They were traveling from Long Island and now they're in Queens." Shoving the iPad in my face, he said "See. Our new drivers have this cool feature similar to Uber where you can follow the car's location. They just made it through Queens."

Placing my hand on his shoulder, I nodded and said "Good work. Text if you need me. Let me greet my guests."

"And the Donor's Achievement Award goes to Mr. David Koch." As I looked around the room at the attendees sitting around the tables, some hiding behind perfectly arraigned flower centerpieces, I stepped aside, pulling Shelly's hand while David took the stand.

"It is with great honor that I accept this distinguished award on behalf of not only myself but the David M. Koch Foundation, my dedicated team, and last but not least my late great grandfather who started this philanthropy. It is with gratitude and appreciation that me, my brother and three sons are able to continue his great work. I look forward to working with New York Presbyterian Hospital for the next decade. Everyone, have a pleasant evening," Koch said as he accepted his award.

We shook hands and posed for the cameras before stepping off the stage. Now that the silent auction had concluded and the Donor's Achievement Award was given out, it was time to celebrate. I motioned over to the bar and ordered a gin and tonic. As I turned to my left, Shelly was standing right next to me, with glossy eyes.

"Must you always drink gin? I would have thought you were an older Irish man, rather than a young sexy black man. It's okay to drink Dusse or Henny at these types of events. It's still top shelf," Shelly teased.

I laughed and grabbed her closer to me, before whispering in her ear. "You know exactly what Henny does to me and this ain't the time nor place."

Shelly chuckled and pulled away from me. "Says who?" She winked and licked her lips.

"Oh, so you're testing me huh?"

"More like teasing you," Shelly moaned as she beckoned me with her index finger.

"Say no more," I told Shelly as I leaned in for a kiss. "Boss man, let me have three shots of Hennessy also," I instructed the bartender who was a gay white guy. Even his eyebrow raised at my request.

"Sounds like an eventful night!"

"Oh, it will be," Shelly interjected.

The bartender placed the drinks on the ledge in front of me and I guzzled down all three shots and sipped on my gin and tonic. My chest sizzled as the cognac made its way down my throat.

"Ahh!" I gasped. Shelly chuckled and started to rub my belly.

We swayed together to the beat of the soft jazz and after fifteen minutes of dancing, the Henny had activated.

"Where's Charlie?" I slurred.

"You gave our girlfriend away to Travis, remember?"

"I didn't give her away, she's still ours."

"Good to know you've forgiven her and come around," Shelly mentioned.

I shrugged and shook my head. "You don't think Charlie's been gaining a little weight?"

Shelly tilted her head to the side and raised her eyebrow. "Haven't really noticed. Why you ask?"

"I don't know, she just looks a bit wider. You didn't notice how her hips were spread out in that dress?"

Just as I said that Charlie waltzed over toward us standing by the bar. She was alone and visibly inebriated.

"What ya'll talking about over here?" Charlie asked.

Before I could help myself, the words fell out of my mouth like water from a canal. "How you've been spreading so much, you almost look like you're pregnant."

17

HORNY BASTARDS

CHARLIE

"**W**ELL, *YOU MIGHT BE RIGHT. FROM HOW HORNY* I feel, it can't just be from the booze," I said in response to Sean's ridiculous assumption. There was no way that I was pregnant, so I didn't even pay his ass any mind. Instead, I grabbed Shelly by the hand and smirked as I stared in Sean's eyes. "Catch us if you can," I said before jolting through the crowd with Shelly in tow.

After several glasses of champagne, I had to leave Travis's side and find my lovers. Shelly was laughing as we made our way to the elevator. Just as we got on it, Sean rushed us and caught the elevator doors from closing. A sexy grin crept up the crevices of his mouth. He was definitely tipsy and the most relaxed I'd ever seen him in public.

"There's no way, ya'll was about to leave me out of the party," he jested.

I laughed and yanked him by the hand until we were face to face and ravishing each other like mad teenagers. Sean kissed me wildly and fondled my breasts out of my dress. Shelly was chuckling the entire time like a drunken bird. As soon as the elevator hit the third floor, Shelly yanked Sean forward then he pulled my hand until we all left the elevator in an assembly line.

Laughing and nearly stumbling over each other, we made our way into one of the exhibits. I squinched my eyes and read *Steichen Galleries* on the door. As we stepped inside, although it was dimly lit, the elaborate reds and greens were still bouncing off the walls. In a matter of a seconds, Sean tore the top of my dress off. The diagonal top fell down and exposed me.

"Ahh, I'm sorry baby. I'm just feigning for you," Sean apologized, as he sucked my neck, getting me even hotter. For a few minutes Sean and I were so lost in each other, that we totally forgot about Shelly until she belted out a low, coy whistle. We turned around and both of our jaws dropped. Standing in the center of two exhibits was Shelly in her birthday suit. The curve of her spine, her tall slender stature, and the dimples in her back illuminated as a sliver of light passed over her.

She swayed back and forth slowly and methodically as if she were begging us to come get her. Looking over her shoulder, she pursed her lips and smooched a kiss. We motioned towards her, Sean getting to her first. Breathing hard and nearly hyperventilating, Sean's hands traveled up and down her body. I watched the bulge in his pants grow, until he was stiff on her back. Dropping down to my knees, I pulled his dick out of his trousers and swallowed it in my mouth. These last few weeks, I was hornier than ever. As I gagged, and choked, distributing enough spit, my pussy got wetter and wetter. Hearing Sean moan turned me on and on, as my nipples hardened.

Sean looked down at me, pleasure written all over his face. His eyes low and his mouth slightly open, I fixated my gaze on him. Kneeling down to a man with his level of power just did something to me. It made me want to please him, especially after his big win tonight. He deserved every suck, I had to give. It's not often you come across a black man of his status who wasn't a rapper or an athlete and I was grateful that Shelly was gracious enough to share him with me. While gawking and looking up at my man with his mouth open, Shelly grabbed his face and continued kissing him. She then rummaged through the buttons on his shirt before tossing it to the side. She bent down and circled her lips around his nipple.

"Oouu, baby you know I love when you do that!" He gasped.

Shelly giggled. "I know!"

I continued to gawk and gawk, allowing his meaty, well-endowed dick to hit the back of my throat. Holding my head firmly, his thrusts were smooth yet becoming harder and harder. As I played with my pussy the moistness saturated my fingers to where they were numb and pruney. Shelly got on her knees beside me and grabbed my pussy scented hand and shoved it in her mouth. She licked my fingers, which turned me on more.

"Wet ass pussy so yummy!" She squealed as she licked her hand profusely, then grabbed me off of her man and kissed me deeply.

After our kiss, she grabbed Sean's dick and swallowed it whole, with no gag reflex at all. She bobbed her head viciously, with no sign of trouble or pain as Sean hummed loudly as if he was in a deep yoga meditation. A moment later he pulled his dick out of Shelly's mouth and splattered semen on both of our faces. Without practicing, Shelly, and I both opened our mouths and caught trickles of his cum. I swooshed it around in my mouth and it was as sweet as sugar gravy. Sean saw the pleasure on my face and grabbed me up by the arm. He quickly turned me around and bent me over. His large hands spread my ass cheeks as he slid his stiff dick inside of me. Moving his hips in circular motions he filled me up.

"Damn, this pussy is just so good. It's so fucking wet!" He moaned as he stroked me over and over again.

With my hands spread out on the floor and my mouth cocked open, tears fell down the side of my face. He was fucking me so good, and he was right, my pussy was wetter than ever.

"Yes, Daddy fuck me!" I shouted and he sped up.

"Yeah, fuck that pussy, Daddy!" Shelly butted in as she lay on the floor playing with her pussy and watching us intently.

Sean glided in and out of my pussy seamlessly like a trained masseuse who massaged every point on your body. I felt like I was about to erupt from the intensifying pleasure, but he beat me to it.

"Arrgh!" He shouted, as he finished and busted his second nut. If we weren't in a polyamorous relationship, where my lovers were millionaires who took care of me, I would have felt like a cheap whore, getting fucked inside of a museum. Instead, I was on a high. While things had gone to shit with Rodney, taking a detrimental unexpected turn, life was only getting sweeter now. Being with the Fox's may not have been the traditional relationship that I was looking for, but it was definitely exciting and beneficial.

My head was throbbing when I woke up and my beautiful champagne-colored dress was laid out across my bed. I didn't want to keep my eyes open. It hurt too much to even blink. I hadn't gotten this drunk in a long time. Since Rodney was a nasty drunk, I stopped drinking while we were together. It turned me off to go to the bar with him or even drink with him at home, especially considering that I was paying for the booze. It turned me off so bad that I stopped drinking totally. I probably hadn't gotten this wasted in two years. It was safe to say that my age was catching up to me.

Elbows on my knees, I held my head in my hands as I sat on the edge of the bed replaying the fragments of last night in my mind. Flashes of Shelly's bare back, and splices of Sean's beautiful dick in my mouth made me tingle a bit inside. My life had turned upside down and around in the matter of a few months. I took a deep breath as I stepped out of the bed. My head was spinning even more now that I was standing. Luckily it was quiet in the house, so I could hear myself think over the airplanes crashing in my head. I walked a few steps toward the door, when Shelly butted in, almost knocking me in the face.

"Good morning sunshine," she greeted me, wearing a long white lace robe. "How are you feeling?"

"As bad as I look."

"You never look bad Charlie," Shelly winked.

I forced a coy smile, as I could never get tired of Shelly's flirting. She knew just what to say to make me feel better.

"I just finished breakfast, wash yourself up and join us," Shelly insisted as she leaned forward and kissed me on the forehead, then the cheek then the mouth. She was so affectionate, and I loved it. I also hadn't realized how much I needed a tender hug and kiss until I met this intimate side of Shelly.

"All right, I'll be out soon," I responded.

She left the room and I scurried into the bathroom adjacent to my room and got myself together. I splashed water on my face to wake me up before brushing my teeth and cleansing my face. It was amazing what Ponds moisturizer could do. Mommy introduced me to the cream when I was a young girl, and it was one thing that I held onto and even swore by.

I stumbled into the kitchen wearing my knee-length silk robe and I found Sean and Shelly both seated on bar stools around the marble island. There were four silver trays in front of them, one with assorted fruit, the others with homemade waffles, turkey bacon and tomatoes, lettuce, and avocado.

"Morning," Sean said flatly. He lifted his gaze to mine and pursed his lips.

"Good morning, babe," I shot back, ignoring his lack of enthusiasm.

I sat down and started to fix my plate. From my peripheral, I noticed Sean and Shelly exchange glances. It was clear they were communicating in code. I continued to fix my plate and finally dug in. The quietness was starting to bug me as the only sound was the shuffling of food on our plates, the impact of Sean picking up and placing down his mug of coffee, and the cool sound of the central air they kept on all the time.

"What ya'll got planned today?" I asked, breaking the silence.

Shelly got up from her seat and before she exited the kitchen, she said "Nothing much. We're resting for a few days. After celebrating such a huge win and all that partying, we're beat."

I nodded my head in agreement. "I understand. I'm beat too. I haven't drunk like that in a while," I explained to myself, and Sean who seemed disinterested in everything I said. How did he go from deep inside me last night to giving me the cold shoulder not even twelve hours later? I thought he had gotten over Rodney threatening Shelly. Especially, since I changed my number and hadn't been receiving any calls from him. I was trying my best to put the Rodney situation behind me, and I was hoping that he had too.

Shelly stepped back into the room holding a few pieces of mail in one hand and a small box in the other. She didn't take any time placing the box down on the island. My eyes zeroed in on the box immediately and saw that it was a pregnancy test. She filtered through the mail and placed a few envelopes on the table.

"Here's some mail for you," she said, avoiding the obvious elephant in the room.

Avoiding my gaze, she pulled a letter out of an envelope. "So, we've got some good news. Our test results came back. We're all clean and tested negative for HIV, Chlamydia, Gonorrhea, Trich, and Herpes Simplex 1 and 2."

"That's a blessing!" Sean piped.

"Yeah, it is!" I added in.

Shelly folded her arms and cleared her throat. "Charlie, we need you to take a pregnancy test!" Shelly demanded.

I scrunched my face as I looked at both of them then glanced over the First Response 2 pack pregnancy test. "Why?"

"Because we think you're pregnant," Sean deadpanned, blinking his eyes twice.

I chuckled and shook my head dramatically. "I'm not pregnant!" I stammered.

"Really? Well, when's the last time you've had your period? You've been here over a month, and we've been fucking nonstop. Don't tell me your period is irregular like Shelly's?"

Shelly's head jerked as she looked at her husband in awe.

I scratched my head then settled my hands on my hips. He was right.

I hadn't had my period since kicking Rodney out.

"Exactly. Take the test!" Sean pressed.

Confusing thoughts swirled in my mind as I thought about the possibility of me actually being pregnant. Jaden was twenty-one years old. I hadn't had a pregnancy scare in the last four years. I had just met Rodney and we slipped up. I lost the baby before I could even abort it. Rodney was distraught considering that he had no children. I was relieved because I refused to bring another baby in the world that I didn't want initially. While I was thankful for my son Jaden, being a teen mother at thirteen was hard and I was forced to have the baby by my parents and Aaron's parents. I was even forced to marry him, even though he was one of the teenage boys who stole my virginity. Our marriage was orchestrated all for the sake of saving face in our southern Georgia community and for his sexual pleasure.

After four years of enduring physical and sexual abuse, I saved up enough money to move to Atlanta and enrolled in Atlanta Technical College. With the help of financial aid, section 8, and public assistance, I was able to keep a roof over me and Jaden's head. I even stripped for two years to afford a divorce attorney. It took a few years to get the divorce settled since Aaron wouldn't budge. Once he finally gave in and the divorce was finalized, I got accepted into the fellowship in New York and me and Jaden left everything behind in our apartment and rode the Amtrak all the way up north. I haven't looked back since or spoken to Aaron, my brother, or my parents. Coming to New York was a fresh start for me and my son. Lord knew we both needed it.

"Babe, if you want me to, I'll come in the bathroom with you. If not, I'll respect your privacy," Shelly said, interrupting my thoughts and handing me the pregnancy test.

Sean still had a screw face painted across his mouth. The only difference was that his arms were folded. This whole time, I was confused as to why Sean was giving me an attitude until it dawned on me. I snatched the test from her and began walking towards the bathroom.

If I was pregnant, there was no telling if the baby was Rodney's or Sean's, because the first time Sean ejaculated inside me was also the same day Rodney raped me.

18
MOTHER NATURE
SHELLY

CHARLIE STEPPED OUT OF THE BATHROOM HOLDING the pregnancy test with disdain riddled on her face. She held it up and it displayed two pink lines. I covered my mouth and stepped back.

"Take the other one!" Sean demanded, with a stern voice.

Without combating, Charlie turned around and stepped back into the bathroom. I followed her and watched her rip the package off the other test and dip it into a stream of urine that sat inside of a cup holstered on the sink. She pulled it out, covered the cap, and allowed it to sit on the sink face up. My hands were twitching and my stomach jittering. I inhaled deeply and exhaled a few times, performing a series of breathing exercises.

After an excruciating minute, Charlie picked up the test and it revealed two pink lines again. I let out a loud squeal, as I was excited, shocked, and overall jovial. We were having a baby.

Sean groaned and kissed his teeth. "Fuck!" He cursed.

"Baby don't be like that. This is so exciting!" I exclaimed.

"For whom?" Sean asked, puzzled. "Doesn't look like Charlie's too excited herself."

Charlie looked at Sean with a menacing scowl and exhaled from her nose. I could see the tension rising in her shoulders. "Excited? Definitely not. I'm still trying to process everything," Charlie whispered.

Sean was holding his head in his hand and fuming. "Same, same, Charlie. In fact, I need some alone time with my wife to process everything and talk through some things. I need you to leave for the day. You can stay at our suite in the Marriott. I'll text you all of the details," Sean said dismissively.

"Sean, no. Absolutely not! We're in this together. We're a family and we're going to handle this as a family!" I interjected.

"Shenelle, do you hear yourself right now? Family? We're not a fucking family. We barely even know Charlie, outside of work. Me and you are family and if she's pregnant with my baby, me and you, wife and husband need to make sense of this together, by ourselves."

"It's funny how you barely know me now, but you had no problem sliding in me raw and nutting in me multiple times!"

Sean rubbed his hands together and an aggravated grin painted his face. "Truthfully Charlie, if it weren't for Shelly taking you in, your ass would have never even been in my home more than once. You're here because Shelly wants you here, not me!"

"THAT'S ENOUGH SEAN!" I yelled.

"You're right that's enough! I'm out of here and I don't need to stay at your suite. I'm gon' let you married folks figure out what you're going to do while I figure out what I'm going to do, because at the end of the day, this is my baby and my responsibility that I'm carrying," Charlie asserted with watery eyes as she scurried out of the bathroom, past both of us.

I followed after her, reaching out to grab her arm and she yanked away from me. "Charlie, wait."

"No, Shelly. Let me go. You go and talk to your husband."

TO BE CONTINUED…

ABOUT THE AUTHOR

Penny Blacwrite is the #1 bestselling author of *Charlie's Angels: A Polyamorous Affair* and the award-winning poetry book *For Every Black Woman's Soul.* Also, she is a published journalist with credits in *Amsterdam News, Our Times Press,* and online entertainment publications *Parle Magazine* and *Enstarz.* Groomed as a student reporter from the age of twelve, Penny was trained by some of the best leading industry writers and journalists from *News Day, 60 Minutes,* CBS, and NBC. Since then, Penny had a knack for storytelling.

As a novelist, Penny writes twisted, forbidden romances, women's fiction and erotica. Nonetheless, she has always longed to tell stories that mirrored her experiences in authentic, creative ways. From being born in prison and raised as a Tupac baby to attending the illustrious Howard University, Penny's real life is the launching pad for her intricate plots, mind-blowing secrets and explosive endings.

Penny is a New Yorker residing in Atlanta with her MacBook, and a mind full of chatter that makes for great stories. Lastly, she is currently studying for her MFA in Creative Writing where she has dreams of launching a specialized niche course focused on self-publishing and rapid releasing at an accredited university.

MAILING LIST

Subscribe to my mailing list for updates, cover reveals and prizes.

PENNY'S READER COMMUNITY

Thank you so much for your continued support! Follow me on the following platforms:

Facebook Group: 5 ★ Page Turners by Penny Blacwrite

Instagram: @pennyblacwrites

Tumblr Blog: For Every Black Woman's Soul

Thank you again.
~Penny Blacwrite